Too good to be true

"You are a good young man," the Pastor Luke Mark John said. "Maybe even the best I have ever met."

"Perhaps you don't know me well enough."

"You'd be surprised how fast I can know such things. I felt your goodness before we even met, and when I *did* touch your hand and see your eyes, it was clear you were special." He gave me a Serious Probing Look, then mocked it with a wink. "There is simply nothing bad about you, Zimmerman. You do nothing bad."

"Perhaps I simply haven't done it yet."

OTHER NOVELS BY BRUCE BROOKS

WHAT HEARTS

EVERYWHERE

NO KIDDING

MIDNIGHT HOUR ENCORES

THE MOVES MAKE THE MAN

ASYLUM FOR NIGHTFACE

BRUCE BROOKS

A LAURA GERINGER BOOK

HarperTrophy®
A Division of HarperCollinsPublishers

Asylum for Nightface
Copyright © 1996 by Bruce Brooks
All rights reserved. No part of this book may be used
or reproduced in any manner whatsoever without written permission except in the case of brief quotations embodied in critical
articles and reviews. Printed in the United States of America. For
information address HarperCollins Children's Books, a division of
HarperCollins Publishers,
10 East 53rd Street, New York, NY 10022.

Library of Congress Cataloging-in-Publication Data
Brooks, Bruce.
    Asylum for Nightface / Bruce Brooks.
        p.   cm.
    Summary: A deeply spiritual fourteen-year-old takes a radical
step to save himself from the fanaticism of his found-again
Christian parents.
    ISBN 0-06-027060-8. — ISBN 0-06-027061-6 (lib. bdg.)
    ISBN 0-06-447214-0 (pbk.)
    [1. Fanaticism—Fiction.   2. Family life—Fiction.
3. Christian life—Fiction.]
I. Title.
PZ7.BZ913As   1996   95-40645
[Fic]—dc20   CIP
                                                      AC

Typography by Hilary Zarycky
First Harper Trophy edition, 1999
❖
Visit us on the World Wide Web!
http://www.harperchildrens.com

ASYLUM FOR NIGHTFACE

O N E

FROM THE STONE doorway of what used to be a dim hardware store and will soon be a bright video rental center, I watch with surprise as the sunlight slants into Ninth Street, reaching between the four-story Wheeler Hotel and the slightly taller spire of the Episcopal church at the east end of downtown, to light up the gutters. The streets are wet. Must have rained last night. Nice sight. But surprising.

I expected no surprises today. This is a day I have planned. It must unfold along

< 1 >

critically placed lines creased in advance. No variables; already thought of everything; I *know* everything. But I did not know to anticipate this rain, which fell while I slept. It is a small thing, it means nothing, it changes nothing. I simply did not think of it in advance. I am angry with myself. But soon enough I realize this may be the effect of nerves; I am not often angry at anyone.

The sun lifts a bit, and the lower edges of the shop windows begin to shine, and now we have moved into the familiar. An alert watcher can see the orderly sequence of illumination, proceeding along the northern side of the street from right to left, as if a silent lamplighter touched a wick at each storefront in turn: the furniture store, the shoe store (full price), the social services agency, the Christian Science Reading Room, the sporting-goods store, the donut shop, the (former) bookstore (now empty, soon to be a chain sub shop), the bank, the coffee shop, the drugstore, the other shoe store (discount), the other bank, and, on the corner, the tavern.

< 2 >

In the middle, between the sporting-goods store and the donut shop, one window breaks the chain, refuses to light up on cue, registers as a dark blip in the center of the sequence. This is because its windows are angled more sharply back from the sidewalk into a deeper doorway: They do not catch the light.

But in just ninety seconds, as if in an afterthought, the sun returns to fix this last spot of night hanging on too long. The angled window is found; its low edge gleams thinly; the line of light grows broader; and the shop joins the rest of the street.

Eventually the light reaches a name stenciled on the window, in red paint over silver foil: *Kollektible Kards*.

< 3 >

T W O

THE MOST PRIVATE ROOM in our house used to be the kitchen. This was unusual, and I knew it. I had seen the movies: The kitchen is where the kids hang out drinking milk and doing homework with yellow pencils while Mom cooks in pots emitting aromatic steam and the flop-eared pooch waits with paws crossed on the floor for scraps. Where the big dinner table with the solid legs and mildly marred surface invites long meals, happy talk, comfortable

< 4 >

company. Where the family's day starts and ends.

Our kitchen was always empty. This was never a forlorn matter. We had talk, meals, company elsewhere. What we did not have was cooking. My mother did not cook in the kitchen, or anywhere. Generally, my father brought food home with him on weeknights—interesting dishes from an ethnic restaurant, crabs or barbecue from streetside vendors, or, when he wanted to be vulgar/hip, fast-food burgers and fries. We ate this food in a dining room at a pale ash-wood table with an unmarred surface, on place mats made of Fitzhugh Lane nautical paintings laminated to white boards edged in gilt paint. The place mats were very nice; it was always sunset, the sky was always clear, the waters were always placid. The plates we used were nice too, from Austria, made of pressed paper of excellent quality, thick and stiff and shiny, light blue one week and custard-yellow the next. The silverware, though plastic, was silvery: It was cast molded of

< 5 >

some brilliant chromelike styrene. The Chardonnay or Zinfandel or Sauvignon Blanc glowed in very thin plastic goblets. After we ate, we threw everything away.

No one went into the kitchen even to wash dishes.

However, I frequently went into the kitchen alone, quietly.

My intention, always, was to pray there. In some ways it was ideal—practically a chapel. First, there was the privacy. My room, where I habitually said my prayers, provided me with a solitude that was only technical. My parents knew I prayed there, and took pains to shuffle back and forth in the hallway whenever my door was shut. They were not actually eavesdropping, but they aimed intense beams of curiosity and alarm through the green-painted wood. In the kitchen, I could have been on my knees for half an hour at a time without the slightest disturbance.

The problem was the floor. The kitchen floor is made up of alternating black and white one-foot squares, in what my parents always insisted was a *chess-*

< 6 >

board pattern. Placing myself on such a square to pray simply invoked too much obvious symbolism ("Just God's little pawn in the game of life!").

I knew that if I belonged to a church that embraced symbol and metaphor (as all churches do), I would have eagerly enjoyed surrendering myself within such a neat bit of allegory ("Move me as you wish, O Father . . ."). But I did not belong to a church—largely because when it comes to my own love of God I dislike symbol, metaphor, and most of all, surrender.

It is ironic that these days my parents are embracing the very things I rejected, including the kitchen floor. When they returned from Jamaica, the kitchen became their favorite spot to fall to their knees with joyous abandon and open the Proclamation of Priority (one of their church's terms for prayer; another is Exchange of Ecstasy). My parents are extremely smart, so it did not take them long to spot and elaborate upon the chess motif. Now they happily speak the homilies right out: "Time to checkmate Lucifer!"

< 7 >

one will exclaim, or "Pawn to God Three: Down with the Black King!"

I sometimes tell myself that if the floor had ever been known as a *checker*-board, I might not have resisted becoming a playing piece. Nobody had ever made grandiose metaphors out of the game of checkers; checkers wasn't anyone's idea of an analog for Life and Strategy. In fact I *like* checkers. Checkers is played with a sense of humor, a tendency to improvise, a no-big-deal adventurousness. But just as my parents would not now insult God by calling him "The Grand Checkers Master," before their conversion they would not have insulted themselves by associating their floor with the inferior game. They were more serious, more subtle, more sophisticated than someone who would have a checkerboard design.

I am happy my parents Exchange Ecstasy with God in The Grand Game. Still, I do not pray with them. My refusal naturally seems like a negative judgment of some sort. Naturally they believe that I—as the family's first Proclaimer of

< 8 >

Priority—ought (at last!) to allow myself to be joined by them, now that they have seen the light.

I have not told them I thought of the whole chess deal two years ago; and I could not now tell them I was—and still am—revolted by it.

< 9 >

THREE

I N 1966, A FIFTH-GRADER in St. Paul, Minnesota, flunked two subjects (arithmetic, reading) for his school's first marking period of the year. These were the only grades below B+ the boy had ever received; he was always an avid student.

His parents were concerned. The boy's mother believed the grades showed he had become lazy and brazen, due to the approach of puberty. She insisted on a cure of toughness, depriving the boy of several privileges she presumed he would

< 10 >

not want to lose—she took away his ice skates and hockey equipment, his radio, his comic books; she cut his allowance; she ceased baking brownies for him every Friday night. As a counterpoint, she also began giving him vast amounts of vitamins A and B and K, in the belief that these would balance the incipient corruption induced by his hormones.

The boy's father felt differently. It had always been the father's private belief that the boy was some sort of genius. All of his life, the child had let out peculiar flashes here and there of startlingly original thought or speech, in the midst of an existence that was otherwise completely conventional and polite. These instances were never disruptive, so they went essentially unnoticed by everyone but the father. But when they were added together and considered—the taking apart and reassembling of a clock at age three; the hobby at age four of reading maps for hours and drawing topographic scenes that were eerily 3-D and eerily representative of geographic elements the boy had never seen;

< 11 >

the ability at age five to mimic the batting stance of nearly every player in the American League two months into the 1961 baseball season after having heard only radio broadcasts of the game—these strange whimsies of outrageous creativity revealed to the father a very interesting kind of intelligence. The father made a point of encouraging all of the little originalities he spotted. For all he knew, the sudden bad grades might be associated with another creative surge.

It so happens that the father owned and operated a large printing business. It was work he loved; he had grown up fascinated by printing, noticing from an early age how incredibly many things in the world had been printed. Naturally, he had always wanted to bring the wondrous arts of printing to his son's attention and, if they intrigued the boy, to put some sort of press at his disposal. Now, as the boy's grades failed to rise despite the vitamins— and as his constant happiness failed to drop, despite the deprivation of skates, money, etc.—the father decided the time

< 12 >

was right. On the next Saturday morning, he would take his son to "the shop." Following a detailed tour of the plant, the boy would be led to a small room stocked with a small letterpress, twelve fonts of hand-set type, various kinds of paper stock, several pounds of ink.

The father was very excited about his plan.

But he was himself in for a surprise.

On the very Saturday morning in question (it was bright and cold, the last leaves were falling, the first snow had not quite come), the boy approached the father— before the invitation had been made to visit the plant—and handed him a cardboard box. Somewhat shyly, but proudly too, he asked his father to take a look at the contents and see if he thought they might be worth printing.

The father opened the box—or, as it is now called, The Box of Boxes, the most famous container in the history of popular illustrated arts in the history of America. Inside were sixty-four comic books, eight sequenced issues of eight different series,

< 13 >

each series featuring a particular super-hero or team of superheroes. At first (he claims) the father believed the books were store-bought—that they had *already* been printed, and the boy simply wanted to reproduce his favorites. The covers were slick paper, the interior pages were news-print; the various institutional insignias were in the right places (company logo, stylized title type, price, copyright infor-mation, etc.); the colors were a little muted and the printing of the speech-balloon type in particular was a bit rough, but for all the father knew this was normal with comics—after all, they were kid stuff, sold for a dime.

But after a minute—aha!—he realized with shock that these books were com-pletely handmade.

Here was the reason for the failing grades.

Here was the seed from which the future of comics would grow.

Here were the first eight issues of *Shockspire, Bad Mind, Lightning and Coolheart, Virtual, Ockenphleck: Knight of*

< 14 >

Bohemia, *No One Knows*, *Tales of Fire and Light*, and *Night Always Follows*. Here were eight worlds, with their own laws of nature, systems of justice, even styles of humor, all coming together roughly but coherently, with astonishing vision and graphic technique. Here, right here, was genius.

The rest, as people say, is history (as is everything about the boy, his father, The Box of Boxes—there have been at least seven books written examining these days). The father took the boy to the printshop that Saturday; soon enough, they were going every Saturday, and almost every weeknight as well. Homework was done, grades were raised, but hockey and radio and brownies were let go. The boy, with his father laying the possibilities of print before him, unleashed his wits and his hand. In a matter of months he had become the greatest underground artist in the history of comics. And, as is so well known now, with the aboveground publication (first in Sweden, then in Japan, then Germany, and so on) of

< 15 >

Why So Deep, a novel-length superhero tale that included holograms and trans-parencies, the boy — now sixteen, now using his name, Drake Jones — emerged as the creator of a new field of literature, or a new art form, or an entirely new popular culture. Everybody knows the rest of the story, everybody knows Drake's creations, you can buy any twelve of his comics in every airport newsstand or bus station.

But there is one small part of the story to examine more closely. It is always over-looked in the new books, and few of even the older historians remember to remem-ber it.

On that first Saturday, when Mr. Jones took ten-year-old Drake in to see the printshop, they did not begin the project of printing comic books on the spot. It was probably Drake who came up with the idea of printing two-sided, two-color trad-ing cards featuring characters from his extended cast of heroes and evildoers. It was certainly Drake who drew the forty-four cardfront images and wrote the forty-four cardback legends; the design and

< 16 >

typography are so sophisticated that these can probably be attributed to his father. What is known is that on a certain Saturday the two of them produced, in a single pressrun, one thousand one hundred and eleven numbered sets of the forty-four cards. They wrapped the sets in printed Mylar wrappers (spot glued), boxed them six to a carton, and took them around to bookstores, newsstands, and hobby shops to be sold; they withheld one set each, numbers 1110/1111 and 1111/1111, but dispersed the rest within weeks. The cards eventually trickled away into the nook-and-cranny world of curiosities. Perhaps Drake had no idea that one day these cards would be the rarest, most prized artifacts in the history of the world of comics. But I think he knew very well. I think Drake had a perfect sense of what would become, well, *kollektible*.

< 17 >

FOUR

IN ALMOST EVERY PAINTING you see of him, Jesus looks like a Swede.

He has long slightly wavy fair hair and luminous blue eyes and a fine straight nose and thin pink lips and long elegant hands. . . . To me this has always seemed like propaganda as much as imagination.

It is true that religion, especially Christianity, is basically a way of letting us love ourselves. That's great. But what we're supposed to have in Jesus is a *person*

< 18 >

with the usual stuff persons have—a body, a mind—who was able, *without becoming more than a person*, to do what he did. To me, the great thing about Jesus is that he was a guy, a human. He wore shoes, he blinked, he itched. And he was able to live as the "son of God." So the last thing I want to do, me personally, is take away his individual identity and turn him into some bleached ideal of what we already accept as Beautiful.

A lot of the Spiffies at my school wear small portraits of Jesus. Every few months the particular form of the jewelry in style changes, but the form of Jesus never does. He's always straight from Stockholm. In the first six weeks of school this fall the favored piece was a small, thick, oval bead painted with his face and set into a gold bezel. It was worn three ways: on a chain around the neck, on a bracelet, or on a pin. One day in geography, I looked at Mary Jersey's pretty pin, then at her pretty face, and said, "You could be his sister. His twin, even."

< 19 >

Mary wasn't sure what to say, but she had a SpifQuip ready. "Well," she said, "I *am* his daughter."

Her sky-blue eyes squeezed slightly into a cautious look. Spiffies are *very* alert to mockery. She said, "But I'm sure you don't mean anything like that, Zimmerman. You *never* mean anything nice."

"I don't mean anything disrespectful," I said.

She rolled her eyes. Janey Larkin, also a Spiffy though not in Mary's church (Janey is allowed to wear lipstick and dance), listened in and said, "Oh, sure, Zimmerman." Janey was wearing a Swede-on-a-bead too.

"Do *you* have a picture of Our Lord anywhere, Zimmerman?" Mary asked.

"Yes," I said. "It's an old painting. It's in my room."

"There's probably something really weird about it," Janey said.

"Yeah," said Mary. "What is it, Zimmerman? What does *your* Christ Jesus look like?"

I took Mary's geography book off her

< 20 >

desk and flipped through it. What I was looking for was in a chapter on the deserts of Syria and Lebanon: a photograph (from 1959) of two men working in a plant that refined dates into sugar. The men were short and thickly muscled, with dark skin, beaky noses, wary eyes under heavy brows, and curly black hair that came low on their wrinkled foreheads. I held out the book to Mary and Janey. "That's what my picture looks like."

Both girls made faces of revulsion, looked at each other, then glared at me. Mary said, "Those are *Arabs.* "

I nodded. "Jesus was born about fifty miles from where these fellows were photographed."

Janey smiled a perfect blank SpifSmirk. "Yeah, well, Christ Jesus was closer to the image of God the Father than other men. He didn't have to look like he came from some *place.* "

In defiant accord, Mary nodded as if she were trying to shake a pebble out of her head through an eye socket. "Yeah," she added. "Christ Jesus came from *Heaven*."

< 21 >

And for the two of them, that was the end of it. They primped their desktops and looked seriously toward the front of the room. Their high cheekbones flushed with holy triumph. Nothing more need be said—they had disposed of the infidel, repelled yet another feeble and petty attack on the citadel of their faith.

But for me, as usual, we had just started to get into something interesting.

On those rare occasions when I have been able to discuss issues of religion, I have found it to be fun. The universe pretty much has all the requirements of a great topic: There is nothing more interesting than Creation, is there?

But no one wants to talk about Creation. I have tried. (Only my friend Marcos would discuss issues of religion with me, even though he had no faith. But Marcos is now in jail, where he has recently been converted to a brand of Christianity that would qualify as Spiffy if it were not represented entirely by murderers and drug addicts and rapists.) Despite my experience with Spiffies, I continue to try to

< 22 >

engage them in talk, but they refuse to come out from behind their slogans. I continue to try, because Spiffies are the only people I know who at least claim to be interested in God and his systems. But Spiffies are not interested in questions. To them, religion is a list of answers. When someone asks a question, they cruise quickly through their mental menu until the right reply-item beeps, then they utter it. All questions are simply a sign of faithlessness: The answer to all questions is simply faith.

Do I believe their faith is "real"? Of course. This is not because I am impressed with them. It is because I am impressed with God. Noticing the design of things and falling in love with it all is not difficult. It requires no special intelligence or compassion or goodness. When Spiffies exude self-congratulation I want to shake my head and say: Why do you feel so smug about yourselves? Finding God is the easiest thing in the world. Anybody can all of a sudden one day say, "Hey, you know, it's pretty cool how I breathe without trying

< 23 >

to," or "It's pretty cool that birds have hollow bones to reduce their weight for flight," or "It's pretty cool how photosynthesis works." The design is not exactly a secret out there. So there's no real reason to act like a spy who just cracked the great code, just because you take note.

In fact, it is my theory that noticing what I call the designing is as involuntary as breathing. We can't *not* do it; our natural curiosity is always sensing orderliness underneath it all, always looking for connections, always being amazed or mystified and then inquisitive. The more you look, the more you find, and the mysteries get clearer but also deeper, and the connections get more interesting, and you just can't stop poking around, until one day you are face to face with the inarguable fact: This is not an accident. This was designed. By a *real* genius.

Then you can do one of two things. You can stop, as the Spiffies (and most churches) do, and say, "Okay, we know enough now, we don't want to hear any more, let's give names to the facts we like

< 24 >

and put a lid on the rest of the mystery box." Or, you can see that you are not smart enough ever to be a threat to the design just by poking around and trying to love *more* of it, and you can keep going.

I want to ask the Spiffies: Why are you so scared?

When I was eight, a family moved in next door to us. They were what I once heard my mother call "foot-washers," which means they were extremely religious Baptists. Not Spiffy ones: They were plain and pious and free of the vanity that makes today's Christian Soldiers cover up their faith with a prideful sheen. But these Baptists were deathly afraid.

Or at least the parents were. There were two boys, one a year younger than me and one a year older. We played all the time. The older one was getting into sports; he taught us how to hit a baseball to him so he could practice catching. The younger one loved insects, so we did a lot of bug hunting. We built a clubhouse in the woods and ate sandwiches there, feeling like we were exploring Antarctica.

< 25 >

But every couple of days the kids would change one of our activities, and it was always a weird change—so weird I couldn't see how they thought of it. For example, the older kid and I had to let the younger kid catch a pop-up for every one that one of us caught, even though he was not very interested in doing so and in fact was kind of afraid of the ball. That pretty much wrecked our baseball practice.

Or this: We had to all of a sudden go around and knock on doors and invite every child in the neighborhood to join our club and use the clubhouse. This brought in a lot of weenies and jerks, and wrecked our club completely.

Then one day the brothers revealed where these crazy ideas were coming from. We had been playing tag a lot with a few other kids. Each game started, of course, with choosing who was It. A nice boy named Jerry rotated around the circle of kids while reciting a rhyme, pointing to each of us in turn as he said each syllable. The rhyme he used was: "Stink in the

< 26 >

barnyard, pee-yooh, Who does it come from? From YOU."

The person who got pointed to when Jerry hit "YOU" was It first.

On this day, when Jerry started his rhyme, the younger brother broke in and said, "My mother doesn't like that rhyme. We can't play unless we use this one." Whereupon he recited a ditty about a choo-choo train and the person who got the last "CHOO!" was It. We all shrugged: Okay, what the heck, let's play tag.

But the change bothered me. I couldn't stop thinking about it. What was wrong with Jerry's rhyme? Why on earth would an adult bother to change it? And more alarming—how had the brothers' mother even heard it?

The questions led me to think about the other changes the brothers had forced on our activities, and soon I got to the bottom of it. The older brother—who had always struck me as uncannily alert and detached—reported everything that happened during the day to his parents. And they considered everything important

< 27 >

enough to evaluate against some sort of standard.

But what was the standard?

I had met the parents and they seemed intensely alert, like the older brother, and carefully nice, like the younger one. The only thing about them that set them off from other parents who were less sensitive and humorless and afraid was their religion.

I had never met any religious people before. I did not know what "religious" meant. But I had heard this family mention the Bible a lot. So I got my grandfather's Bible down from the "retired bookshelf" in the basement, as my father called it, and started to read. I was a slow reader at eight, but a good one. I spent a lot of time reading this book. It was pretty good, when it wasn't incredibly boring. I skimmed a lot of the historical material; what I was really looking for was the passage that said you had to do what the Baptist family was doing.

I never found anything that dictated an attitude of constant sweetness. In fact,

< 28 >

most of the people in the Bible—and God, too—don't hesitate to *hammer* competitors, enemies, etc. This made me wonder if people like the Baptists (and the Spiffies today) act all sweetsy because deep down they're afraid of being naturally kind of mean.

Actually, I think it's more that they're afraid of doing something Wrong. I have heard a lot of Spiffies say that every word in the Bible must be taken literally and followed literally. This could get pretty scary. A lot of weird people proclaim things in the Bible. Do you believe *all* of them?

I suppose this is why people turn their personal wits over to their preachers—so the preachers can decide what the "literal" meaning is, and tell them what to do.

I figured this out: In any book or prayer or sermon, part may be said to come from God, but most comes from a human being trying to put God into words. Human beings have opinions and fears and struggles with other human beings also trying to put God into words. It is up to us to take what seems good and shrug at

< 29 >

the rest. I think we are supposed to do the same with the world.

It would be nice if I could say that my investigation of the Bible is what initiated my interest in Creation, the designing, God, etc. But it isn't. If anything, finding so much proclamation made me a little skittish. So I put the Bible away, and tried *not* to think about such things for a while. Instead, I turned to comic books.

< 30 >

FIVE

KOLLEKTIBLE KARDS is a stupid name.

Standing in the street, looking at the silver-and-red sign, I am aware that in a small way, the stupid name may have helped make possible my decisions to do what I will do today. I acknowledge that I may have been very slightly influenced by my feelings for the spirit behind those ridiculous K's.

This is wrong.

My reasons should be clear without the intrusion of such a dishonorable feeling

< 31 >

as scorn. I hope that I am acting only out of honor, difficult though that honor may be to explain.

Standing in my doorway, I consider the entire plan in light of this admission. It takes me a few minutes. The reasons stand.

I look at my watch. In six minutes the door of the donut shop will be opened, by a man named Jack Waller. Age: 51. Height: about 5´6˝. Weight: about 190 pounds. Jack Waller will park his 1987 Chevrolet Citation (white, with a dented front right fender) in a small space at the rear of his shop, and walk through a tight alley that brings him out slightly east of the shop's doorway. He does this to leave the parking places on the street free for customers coming for his baked goods, or indeed for the things vended by any of his neighbors.

Jack's father opened the donut shop in 1933. Jack has worked there since 1950, when he was six and first learned to spread chocolate icing on blank donuts. He wants to turn the shop over to his own

< 32 >

son, Jackie, now aged nineteen. Jackie, like his dad, has grown up among the wonderful aromas of fresh fried dough and boiled glazing sugar. But for the past eight years Jackie has cared only for the aroma of polypropylene glue; at the moment he is in his sixth stay at a state substance-abuse treatment center. It is said he no longer has a head for the business. Here comes Jack.

It will be almost an hour before the next shopkeeper arrives. After that, they will show up at intervals of six, eleven, two, two, five, twenty, twenty-one, and six minutes. The arrival of the last shopkeeper is unpredictable.

His name is Mason Farwell. He is the half owner of Kollektible Kards.

The K's, as it happens, were entirely his idea.

< 33 >

SIX

MY PICTURE OF JESUS is actually very nice. It is a reproduction of a full-figure portrait in a style of painting that I believe is now called superrealism. I cannot imagine it was called such a name when this picture was painted. I have seen a wonderful example of this style in the Museum of Modern Art in New York City: a very small portrait of Gala, his wife, painted by Salvador Dali. No matter how closely you look, you cannot find evidence of a brushstroke anywhere; there is no artistic

< 34 >

surface. In a way, the painter has chosen to disappear. But, boy, do you get a good look at Gala.

You get a good look at Jesus in my picture. Short, with dark hair and eyes, beardless, he is standing on a dark path in the woods, looking as if he has just come to a quick halt from a tense walk, arrested by the flash of a photographer's bulb. He faces "the camera" simply, hands at his side, shoulders slightly forward, weight on the balls of his feet; poised for a moment as if obligated to allow his picture to be "taken."

He is not smiling. He does not look as if he is about to bless you and give you something nice to eat. In fact, his eyes look kind of annoyed and suspicious, his mouth straight but on its way to a small frown, his forehead wrinkled in worry or irritation or fatigue. It is clear he thought he was alone in the woods but has better manners than to ask, "Who are you and why do you bother me while I meditate?" You can see, too, that he is used to being interrupted, used to being alone only

< 35 >

rarely. He looks pretty tired of company. (If you have read the New Testament, you can certainly see why.)

I like thinking about Jesus as an amazing man. A man who was smart, generous, tough, compulsive, brash, almost crazy in his commitment to something hard to share, certainly intense to the point of being frightening, and definitely, definitely tired. Also, lonesome, the way private people are when surrounded by others less ingenious.

My picture accepts these qualities. At least it does not hide them. It does not pretend Jesus is above being a human being, the way other pictures (and churches) do. In other portraits, Jesus is extraordinary. His untroubled beauty and bliss radiate the message that he is different from us all. Different, and better.

I always wonder: How will a person who goes to one of these churches feel when Jesus is held up to him as "a man," but a man who never got tired or arrogant? It is pretty difficult to feel such a man is of the same species we are. It is difficult to

< 36 >

feel that sort of aspiring kinship that lets us say, "Yes, I see—with some insight and some discipline and some luck, I could be a good guy too!" Instead, faced with Jesus's impossible blue-eyed bliss, we are moved to say, "No way I could get to *that*."

Jesus was not some kind of angel. Jesus was a man. That was the *point*, wasn't it? Of being born? Of dying?

< 37 >

SEVEN

THE CHRISTIAN SECT into which my parents were indoctrinated in Jamaica is called Faith of Faiths. An interesting name; it manages to sound both arrogant and humble at the same time. Among initiates, my parents sometimes refer to it as "Double-F," but this is only for those who have earned the right to be familiar.

Frankly I don't know what to call it. "Your faith" sounds incomplete, abbreviated. "Your religion" is too broad, and formal, and excluding; after all, they have adopted

< 38 >

the religious classification "Christian" just as I have. And there is no physical, architectural center that symbolizes the sect, so it would be inaccurate to refer to "your church."

Upon their return, my parents were happy to blurt out the story of their "awakening," from which I was able to piece together an outline of the sect's techniques for recruiting members. (After a few days, my parents grew quieter about the matter, to the point that any inquiry of mine was deflected with a polite kind of wariness.)

The recruiting process is a brilliant one. I am impressed with the strategic sense of Luke Mark John, the founder of Faith of Faiths. He has selected a clearly defined pool of candidates (upper-middle-class patrons of elite Caribbean resorts), studied their habits (drinking and eating and sleeping too much, leading to exasperation, discomfort, and guilt), and created a product (instant austerity and self-respect) expressed within an ideology (his particular brand of abject Christianity) that is both

< 39 >

familiar and almost laughably weird in the personal sense ("Us? *Christians?* Like those ignorant Pentecostals with bad teeth, howling in the hills of Tennessee? What an idea!") that exploits the yen for something-new/adventure people exercise on vacation.

Basically, what happens is this: On the Thursday morning of each week, his bright disciples wander from the beach into the open-air breakfast buffets that are a required feature of the resorts, and insinuate themselves into coffee conversations with the patrons. The puffy, hungover vacationers look on the chipper, healthy model types with appreciation and envy ("I wish I felt that good . . ."). Eventually the disciple is asked what the secret is—and lo and behold! It's not sun and leisure and good nutrition, but a simple matter of Ffaith!

The program gets very efficient here; once again I admire Mr. John, this time for his restraint. To the Puffies, the model lightly summarizes the benefits of his religious practice. But, um, it's, well, kind of

< 40 >

hard to describe, really. But—wait! Here's an idea!—he invites the Puffies to take a stroll on the beach, where they *may* just encounter some fellow advocates of the Faith. Which they do, along with other tagalongs like themselves. Next thing you know, a kind of "spontaneous" seminar takes place right there on the ivory sand, and before you know it—why, here comes Luke Mark John himself (in Jams and a T-shirt and sunglasses, with a towel over his arm). Next thing you know, everyone kind of decides to give rebirth a try, just kind of a lark, nothing *serious*. . . . But the next couple of (non-indulgent) days prove incredibly refreshing, and Creation looks pretty good down on those islands, and they decide they want to meet again with some of the Ffaithful. But they are nowhere to be found!

As they are leaving on Saturday, though, who should be at the airport but a few of the models and Mr. John himself, ready with a makeshift-looking packet of materials and a quick little ritual of acceptance into membership ("It's kind of a

< 41 >

club, really, not so much a religion or any-thing . . . "). Credit cards accepted.

Luke Mark John sounds like a pretty hip fellow, playing his role with easy humor, casual intelligence, unassuming power. My parents are careful to stipulate that they do not idolize or worship or revere this man, from which I gather that he has made a point of declining such obeisance with grand humility.

"We worship only The Christ," my mother has insisted, several times, always using the definite article.

"Right," my father says. "Luke Mark John is merely His *avatar*."

My mother nods, but is uncomfortable leaving Mr. John embodied coldly in such a strange word, modified only by *merely*: "We are allowed to *love* the avatar," she says, blushing. My father blushes too. "Out of *respect*," he adds.

All right. It happens that I have a the-ory that all love is the same, and is essen-tially a love of God. I'm not completely sure this can be said without some qualifi-cation, but basically I think it fits. So put

< 42 >

banana custard, or your girlfriend, or base-ball, or one's mom and dad, or dawn on a clear December morning, or the geometry of a parallelogram, or superheroes, or Luke Mark John into the world—and when you love one of these things, you are loving the design, or a part of it. And loving any part of it is really loving the whole deal. Okay.

I remind myself that the joy of discovering God may not be contained so simply in the word or idea of, well, some genius designer out there. I recall that we are used to attaching joy and love to *people,* and that if Christ (who was made for the purpose) still seems kind of abstract, then, fine, the feelings will associate themselves with someone near at hand, especially someone who was involved in the awak-ening of this blissful discovery. Right?

So it may well be that in a while— another few months, perhaps—the giddy reverence my parents now keep feeling for this "avatar" will instead turn naturally to God. *Then* we can talk about many great things together; *then* we can enjoy

< 43 >

Creation with no ambiguity about who is responsible for our joy; *then* we can happily analyze and argue without fear. I must be patient. It is entirely possible my parents and I will spend a lifetime harmoniously recognizing the same basic things. If it takes a while for us to realize we have arrived at the same place, well—so what?

< 44 >

EIGHT

MARCOS AND I KNEW each other for a long time despite the fact that he is three years older. As a rule, older kids are too cool to notice younger kids; rascally troublemakers are too cool to notice benign dweebs, too. But Marcos loves going against the rules.

One day when I was in the fifth grade he came up to me at lunch and said, "You know, I always hated your guts, but I have finally realized you are just as lonely as me." Then he sat down and ate without

< 45 >

saying another word. After that we found ourselves together a lot.

For a long time, Marcos was the only one who knew I had fallen in love with God. At the time that I told him, both of us were also in love with a girl named Patrice, who was exactly between us in age. We were openly competing for her affection. Somehow it did not threaten our friendship, and to her credit Patrice did not try to play us against each other. She liked us both pretty much, and was certainly fair. But although Patrice had held out for a while against Marcos's obviously superior vitality and snazzier potential, I knew it would not be long before she chose him.

I did not want Marcos to feel bad about winning Patrice over me, so one day while we were walking in town I told him everything. He scoffed at my wussiness for pulling out of the competition. But he decided not to scoff at my feeling for God.

"Just don't ever try to get me interested," he said.

"You *are* interested," I said.

"I'm interested in *you*. You're pretty

< 46 >

weird. But I'm not interested in God worth a frog hair."

"God can be pretty weird too. Or he can *seem* pretty weird. But really, see, it's all kind of worked out so that—"

"You're doing it already," he said, turning in the other direction. "I'm going to go try to kiss Patrice. Sure you don't want to get in my way?"

"I'm sure."

"Then good-bye."

Strangely enough, Patrice and Marcos did not appear to get together. Marcos never mentioned the situation, so I never knew. Soon, though, instead of devoting himself to a single girlfriend he showed a preference for being hounded by many girls of different sorts, in overlapping waves of ardor, jealousy, etc. In the eighth grade, at least two of the girls associated with Marcos became pregnant. We never talked about that, either.

In the seventh grade I meandered into a quiet relationship with a girl named Monica, who was intelligent but unimaginative. For me, for our friendship, she felt

< 47 >

a profound, loyal fondness, but not a passion. This was fine with me. I was still pretty mystified by the prospective consequences of passion. Though I did not necessarily subscribe to biblical prohibitions, I did feel such mysteries might make more sense after one was married. This was a pretty difficult thing to adhere to, among the people in my school—especially as Marcos was my best friend.

Once Marcos and I were talking at his locker, when a girl named Sahndra walked up, cut between us, squeezed her back against the locker door, then pushed her chest out so that her breasts were just touching Marcos's T-shirt.

"You're not going to ignore me," Sahndra said with a pout that changed into a crafty smile.

This was a pretty typical intrusion. Marcos and I were used to snatching chats in between such encounters with girls; he had long since stopped apologizing, and I had long since learned to withdraw with the knowledge that we would meet later and pick up where we left off.

< 48 >

But this time something different happened. As I stood there for a two-beat to make sure Marcos was not going to tell Sahndra to go away, someone put her hands into both of my pants pockets from behind. I froze, and a voice close to my ear said, "Does Marcos's friend get as lonesome as Sahndra's friend? Does he wonder what they do together?"

I spun around by instinct. This was not a kind thing to do: The girl—her name was Peri—did not have time to remove her hands from my pockets, and my spin bent her wrists harshly. She shrieked a curse and tugged them free and stood there glaring at me as she rubbed them. Marcos and Sahndra, who had already started walking away, turned and looked.

"What's up?" said Marcos.

"Your friend isn't," snapped Peri. Then she gave a nasty little laugh and looked at me with a kind of flashing mockery. "He doesn't know the difference between a woman's hands on his crotch and a spider."

"Maybe he thinks there's *not* a whole lot

< 49 >

of difference," said Marcos. He had dropped Sahndra's hand and taken a small step back toward us. Sahndra was holding him by the chest and murmuring.

"That's sexist," said Peri.

Marcos laughed. "You brought up the comparison."

Peri looked at me. She shook her head sadly. "Whoever would have thought the great Marcos would have a sexless weenie for a friend?"

Marcos was not far away—maybe eight feet—but even so I was surprised by how quickly he arrived to push his face into Peri's and walk her backward three, four, five steps. He stopped, pushing right against her, and she stopped too. Marcos stared into her eyes. She looked afraid, and defiant, and also something else I couldn't identify.

"You wouldn't understand honor," said Marcos. He smiled.

Peri smiled back. "No," she said.

Marcos fastened his mouth over hers. It would be inaccurate to call it a kiss. Their mouths were open but clamped

< 50 >

tight like two pipes joined for a flow of waste water. Peri leaned into Marcos a little. Sahndra gave a cry behind us. Peri's hands started to slide up Marcos's arms.

He suddenly pulled his mouth away. Peri's was open and lunging—I saw her pink tongue flicking outward—and she was startled. Marcos took a step back and grabbed one of her hands in his and jammed it against his pants.

She gaped.

"See?" he said. "Me, too. Just like my buddy."

"You—"

"Only in my case it's not honor," he said. "It's just that I don't like you. I'll tell you something: I don't really understand honor any more than you. But I recognize it. I respect it. And you better do the same." He flung her hand away.

"Let's go," he said to me. We walked away. Ten seconds later, calmly, he resumed our talk from the point at which it had been broken off.

From time to time Marcos would ask me if I had dug up any interesting things

< 51 >

about God lately. I would gratefully launch into a detailed summary of whatever investigations I had been pursuing, and he would listen with care, often raising clever contrary points. I don't know what Marcos got from these; he was always thoughtful and precise, but nothing he said revealed any reading or research or previous thought. There was no evidence that he took anything away from our talks, or brought anything to them—except an interest in me.

Once we were sitting on the leaves along the edge of the field where we sometimes kicked a soccer ball back and forth. It was probably October; I remember our breath showed in the chilly air, but the light from the sun in the west still brought an idea of warmth.

"Hey," Marcos said. "Question."

"What?"

He looked up at the tree above us, then over across the field, where a woman in a purple coat was walking a golden retriever. Then he looked at me. "Did Jesus ever lose it?"

< 52 >

"You mean, like, get so mad—"

"—that he forgot to be Mr. Sweetness, Son of God. Yes. Did he?"

"Yes. At *least* once. Maybe more times, but it's not the kind of thing his followers would want to write up for the Book of Ages. I mean, for instance, maybe he blew them away every time they didn't do a good job on one of the assignments he gave them. But telling on him would make him look bad, and them too."

Marcos nodded. "Image is everything. But you say there is one story in the Holy Marketing Manual?"

"Yes. In this one temple, the town's moneylenders had set up tables where they did their business. Local custom. It was a good spot to catch customers, I guess. So, one day Jesus hits town, goes to the temple, and sees this thriving financial center. He picks up a whip and goes nuts, thrashing around, scattering all the coinage, knocking over tables. A genuine rage."

"Kicking a little godless tail," Marcos said, with an appreciative whistle. "But imagine what it did to interest rates."

< 53 >

I laughed. After a few minutes during which we both watched the golden retriever fetch sticks, Marcos said, "Maybe it wasn't completely a bogus idea, having the money booths in the temple."

"What do you mean?"

He shrugged. "You go to the temple to worship what you love, right?"

"Well," I said, thinking, "that's actually a pretty good general definition—"

"Well, there's never been a time when people didn't love wealth." He held up a finger and looked at me warningly. "And I'm *not* making some goody-goody point about how 'it's just awful in these materialistic times that we place such value on fleeting worldly chucketa chucketa chucketa.' Frankly I see nothing wrong with being rich. But if I recall correctly from my three visits to Sunday School at age five, before I turned to a life of sin and lawlessness, there's quite a bit of stuff from J.C. about how rich guys can't enter heaven, easier to go through the eye of a needle, such stuff." He shook his head. "Frankly, I was amazed to hear they *had*

< 54 >

needles back then."

From this conversation it may seem that Marcos was enquiring because *he* was in love with wealth. But I don't believe he was. I say this even though he possessed a great many expensive things (nice car, several Fender guitars, excellent boots and coats and ice skates) and obviously devoted a certain amount of craft to the task of securing lots of money. I believe Marcos was one of those people who go after money because they know it is out there to be gotten by *someone*. The pursuit can be a kind of game. An adventure.

Unfortunately, it was a game Marcos lost, not long after our talk about Jesus and the moneylenders. The day before Thanksgiving Marcos was caught selling a half pound of apparently superb home-grown hybrid marijuana to a customer in front of an undercover law enforcement agent who had been preparing to bust him for months. Actually, the agent was on the site—a fountain festooned with angel statues in a corner of our local park, a well-known spot for illicit markets—to make a

< 55 >

purchase from Marcos himself. But before he could do so, another man came up and transacted a deal under his nose, and the agent had his bust.

Unluckily for Marcos, as it turns out, the assistant district attorney in charge of prosecuting happened to be the uncle of one of the girls who had become pregnant in the eighth grade during her association with Marcos. Also, as luck would have it, the city's best defense attorney—quite famous for his arrogance and cunning—was unavailable to represent him. The reason for this was simple: It was this defense attorney who had made the purchase of marijuana in front of the drug agent.

Naturally, the prosecutor counted himself triply blessed. Here was a chance to wreak revenge on many levels at once. Marcos was tried as an adult though he was still a juvenile, and sentenced to several years in a state prison. The prosecutor managed to portray him as an evil power bent on corrupting our society's upstanding professionals, as represented by the fallen attorney—a neat reversal of the

< 56 >

usual adult-corrupting-youth bit.

I was sorry to see Marcos go to prison. But frankly I did not mind the youth-corrupts-adult angle as much as I might have, because, as it happens, the defense attorney who bought the marijuana was my father. He received a suspended sentence and a long probation. His practice barely suffered; juries seemed to like him better than ever now. And his probation turned out to be pretty loose. He was even allowed a special release to take a vacation in Jamaica six months ago, before a year had elapsed.

I wrote letters to Marcos, every other day for the first few weeks. He answered every couple of weeks, each of his notes containing a couple of hilarious anecdotes about the absurd horrors of life in jail. He wrote nothing about himself; one was left to infer from his cheery point of view either that he was doing all right, or, equally likely, that he was being crushed but wished to hide behind a pose of good cheer.

Then his letters stopped coming. For

< 57 >

almost three months I heard nothing from him.

I continued to write to him. I did not refer to his silence. I figured that he wasn't going to disappear on me—I knew where he was. There was no real worry.

One day I got an envelope addressed in Marcos's hand, from the prison. I opened it. Inside, there was no letter; instead, I found a neatly printed little document, folded twice to the size of a trading card. On the front was Marcos's smiling face. Beneath his neck was a small headline that said I FOUND HIM AT THE BOTTOM OF A NICKEL BAG. The rest of the printing spelled out a brief tale of sin and redemption starring a character bearing Marcos's name but few of his qualities. I frankly expected to see some reference to myself—in such a narrative, there is a ready-made role for the friend who brings news of the Savior and so forth—but I made no appearance. News of the Savior was brought, in Marcos's tale, by a double murderer who came back to life after hanging himself with a pillowcase, because Jesus called

< 58 >

him to share His gospel.

Across the bottom of the final panel—right below the printed closing line "And may my story of salvation inspire you to see that each nickel bag costs your soul more than its worldly worth!"—Marcos had written me a message.

Well, he wrote, there's nothing else to do here. And P.S.—I know, I know—it was a half lb., not a "nickel bag." My best to your pop.

< 59 >

NINE

SOME OF THE PEOPLE in my school feel
they barely know their parents. In most
cases this is because their parents work
hard at their jobs. These "kids" respect
their parents in a general sort of way, and
feel a broad if sometimes vague gratitude
for their upbringing, or at least for their
home and possessions. But in talking to
them, I perceive that they do not have
especially deep or detailed ideas of their
parents as individuals.

This is not the case with me. It is true

< 60 >

that both of my parents have always worked, with diligence, satisfaction, and concentration. In our home, at least until recently, my father's law practice and my mother's radio advertising agency have held a legitimate, primary importance.

But this does not prevent me from knowing who my mother is, and my father. On the contrary, seeing them performing their work gives me another angle from which to deduce aspects of their nature. Watching my dad in court taught me a lot about his cleverness, sense of drama, compassion, and ruthlessness. Listening to my mother's advertisements on the radio taught me just as much about her wit, craftiness, aesthetic principles, and honor.

I liked what I learned. I have always been proud of them. Have they ignored their responsibilities as parents because of their professional dedication? By no means. Their attentiveness to me has always been constant, specific, concerned. True, they have not always been happy with what I do; but they do not prohibit or

< 61 >

curtail. They offer alternatives, encourage different behavior, but my liberty is never impeded.

My parents granted me the right to fall in love with God and the designing.

They were not at all pleased with my subsequent straightness. But they did not attempt to coerce me out of it. Cajole, yes; argue, definitely; display frustration and perhaps even fear, absolutely. But coerce? Never.

So I never tried to coerce them in return.

Certainly, it never occurred to me to try to "save" them. Such audacity is, I hope, not within my nature. It is for each of us to follow his or her intuition and curiosity deeper and deeper into Creation blah blah blah. You can't just tell someone about Creation, however loudly, and expect the devotion to spring forth, any more than you could tell a girl about some great guy and expect her to say, "Fine, I'll marry him right away, no problem!"

I worried from time to time that I might have hurt my parents' feelings by

< 62 >

not making an effort to share my appreciation with them. I believe they expected such an effort; these days most people who call themselves "Christian" (or even "religious") subject anyone they meet to a dreaded all-smiles harangue and an I'm-only-trying-to-share! harassment.

Frankly, I have expected this sort of thing from my parents since they returned from Jamaica with their new faith. I wait for the too-bright smile or the I'm-worried-about-you knitted-brow frown or the fake-casual tone that usually opens such approaches. And when these fail to materialize, I *do* feel a little disappointed, even hurt, despite my relief. There is just a moment when something inside me says, "Don't they care?"

Have my parents been saying this all along, for years? Was their fearfulness and crankiness about me just a resentment of my refusal to share? Were they always waiting for me to speak, even to beckon? Were they always ready for faith? Would they have dropped the Chardonnay and the dope and the deception in their work,

< 63 >

all for God—through *me*, instead of through L. M. John?

I do not think so, really. I feel bad saying this, but—I don't believe my parents would have considered joining in a belief first discovered by someone else in their life. My parents always proudly declared that they were not "joiners." Joining was perilously close to being "derivative."

"Derivative" was not a nice word in our house; it was spoken only with contempt. Any type of thing could bring it forth: a song on the radio, an automobile's roof line, a third baseman's batting stance, the toe hole of a patent-leather dress pump, a cupola on a new building, a dill-and-shallot sauce on a piece of steamed bass—my parents were always alert to nuances betraying an inspiration drawn from the familiar. Sometimes, in a museum or store, they would scold a piece of derivative work to its face. "Think yourself!" they would say to a painting by a lesser Fauve, or a nouveau-Deco pitcher, then turn away with a dry laugh and a wave of dismissal.

Once my parents spent several hours

< 64 >

shuttling between a swank Italian furniture "studio" and a diner around the corner, deliberating about whether or not to buy an ottoman. They had already decided to buy a chrome-and-black-leather sling chair from the studio—a chair that rotated and reclined through the agency of various joints and gears, also chrome, located in the open between the seat and base. These "visible mechanicals" represented the latest thinking in the Milanese avant-garde, according to the "studio consultant." My father, sitting in the chair one last time after agreeing to buy it, happened to mention that he liked to put his feet up, a pleasure he guessed he would have to give up. But no! said the salesman, who slipped away and was back in ten seconds with a small black-leather-and-chrome ottoman that seemed perfectly to match the chair. My father sat back, rested his feet on it, and sighed happily.

Unfortunately, instead of simply buying the ottoman, my mother asked why it was not displayed with the chair.

The consultant confessed it was

< 65 >

because the ottoman had not been created by the same designer.

My parents frowned. Not the same designer. But so similar in design and material—right down to a few exposed chrome gears—that one could hardly escape the suspicion that a concept had been, well, borrowed.

My parents smelled derivation.

They did not buy the derivative ottoman. And so disturbed were they by the infection of derivativeness, they passed on the chair as well.

It took hours to make this decision, but one couldn't be too careful about such things.

Were these two people likely to buy a well-used religion from a kid? I doubted it.

< 66 >

T E N

THE APOLOGIES BEGAN three days after my parents returned from Jamaica. For those three days, I sensed a very slight but growing unease in the way they regarded me.

The change was mostly a matter of a mysterious kind of deference.

Although my parents have not made me feel unloved, they *have* been explicit with the mild scorn they felt for what my mother called my "bleached lifestyle" of the past three years. (The laundry motif

< 67 >

was a popular one with her: Once, when her own breath was especially redolent of retsina, she said, "Zimmie, you know, you are so clean your breath smells like fabric softener.") Before my bleaching, their ardor for me was clear and complete— which does not make me feel I have lost their love, but, rather, makes me certain I still have it beneath the surface uncertainties all of this godliness has brought. I only need to think for an instant to remember my mother picking me up from a muddy clump of leaves in a rainy gutter, and kissing my grubby face again and again, until she had as many leaves stuck with goop to her own face as I did; to remember my father plucking me from the grocery cart in supermarkets and hugging me to him, unable to roll another ten feet without doing something with his love for me, sighing happily, groaning sometimes with what I could see even at age three was joy, joy, joy; to remember the two of them sitting cross-legged on whatever low surface I sat on, as I drew unintelligible shapes with crayons, or pulled an earthworm out

< 68 >

of the ground, or dug at the surf line after sand fiddlers, or ate the grapes I had purposefully spilled on the floor.

They have always respected me. But there is a difference between respect and deference.

This deference was expressed as soon as they got off the plane, in a gesture I regarded at the time as some kind of ironic joke: My father ran up the last few yards of jetway and fell on his knees in front of me, looking up into my eyes with a supplicant's reverence.

I was humiliated and furious; I thought he was mocking me again, though that had usually been my mother's role. But before I could think of what to say, my mother ran up behind him kind of cringing, with her hands clasped earnestly, and looked at me with the same eyes. "Dear Boy," she intoned (a phrase I had never heard in my life), "we have found Him at last."

"And," said my father, "in finding Him we recognize that we have been losing Thee."

This was all so weird that I realized

< 69 >

only later that it must have been a prepared speech; at the moment I could
think only of hauling my father back to
his feet. But he was glancing over his left
shoulder as if his chin had been yanked
by a wire.

Coming up behind them, ignoring my
parents and looking only at me with an
amused and familiar eye, was a small
man with a trim beard, gold glasses with
perfectly round lenses worn low on his
nose, and a beat-up straw hat that looked
expensive despite its raggedness. My
father rose to his feet, hands still clasped.
I was forgotten.

"Very good," the man said, in a peculiar voice. It was both whispery and
jovial, an unusual combo. I realized that
he was approving my parents' perfor-
mance, though he had not taken his eyes
off me. My father relaxed his shoulders,
my mother straightened up just a hair.
The man smiled at me—with a slightly
conspiratorial glimmer, as if we both knew
my parents were being a bit ridiculous
but should be humored because we loved

< 70 >

them (which was pretty much how I, at least, was feeling). Looking suddenly like a secure, warmhearted, slightly daffy French Impressionist painter greeting a colleague, he extended both his arms at waist level. The gesture neatly parted my parents, each of whom took a hasty step backward.

Not knowing what else to do, I put *my* hands out. The little man took them lightly in his and gave a couple of casual shakes. My parents gasped, and looked across him at each other with a kind of rapture.

"Nice to meet you, Zimmerman," said the man. "I'm Luke. I've heard a great deal about you from your excellent mother and father. And I just wanted to thank you personally for"—he chuckled—"let's see, shall we say 'softening them up' for the past few years?"

"What are you talking about?" I said. My parents winced.

Luke did not; his smile got merrier, and one eyebrow rose. "Well, the only thing I *ever* talk about—the joy of bringing people into my faith."

< 71 >

So it was that I had the privilege of meeting (and being touched by—"He *never* touches *anyone!*" my father jabbered later, again and again)—the founder of Faith of Faiths. On the way home from the airport, after Luke (I have since learned his previous name was Gerald Covington) had said a few chummy/cryptic things to me implying that the two of us knew many things we wouldn't speak of just now and strolled back down the jetway to resume his seat for another destination, my parents breathlessly explained to me that he had met them at the airport in Kingston and asked (*Asked! Such humility! As if anyone would ever say no!*) if they would mind (*Mind!*) his company for the first leg of their flight. As they told the story, they leaned excitedly over the seat between them and interrupted each other happily, like harmonious siblings reiterating a thrilling encounter to each other, using the present parent (me in this case) as a pretext for sharing their private joy.

Their giddiness did not abate in those first days. They chattered and chuckled and

< 72 >

shouted their new slogans and laughed over recollections of their fellow inductees, at all times of day, anywhere in the house, almost always following such celebrations with a long, fervent, full-voiced prayer. (They explained that Luke, whom they called The Pastor John, claimed that praying in silence was timid, "a kind of hiding in shame." Perhaps that is why he left Matthew out of his name: That book in the New Testament contains Christ's harsh words for those who show off their piety by praying in public.)

They performed all of this joyousness in my presence. But, just as in the car, their affirmation did not exactly *include* me; they were really talking to each other while I happened to be around. This was just fine with me.

But then, in the middle of one of their rhapsodies, my father would jerk his head up and look at me with sudden, fearful sobriety. A meaningful glance at my mother would follow; and for the next half hour the two of them would pay earnest attention to me, eyes wide open, heads

< 73 >

slightly inclined, with frequent nods whenever I spoke. And after the half hour, they would exchange another Significant Look, and my father would clear his throat and launch an Apology.

The form was always the same. "My Son, we have much to be sorry for," he would say, sounding like a parody of a common Christian prayer of thanksgiving. Then, overriding my protests (which I soon abandoned), he would proceed to express pretty precise feelings of shame for one of many instances in which they had failed to honor my stunning foresight in finding "The Christ Jesus" years ago.

For many reasons I hate the Apologies.

For one thing, they are not exchanges, or even communications. There is nothing natural about them. The people standing there have nothing in common with my real father, my real mother, my real self. This man speaks a scripted passage; this woman bows her head in humble guilt; this boy fumes awkwardly. I have no doubt that my parents do feel bad about having given me a hard time for beliefs

< 74 >

they now approximate. Okay, no problem, that's over. Can we move on now? No. Atonement must be made, and made, and made.

Once I tried saying, "Only God deserves atonement." They gaped at me with an even worse worshipful awe ("Did you hear *that*? Such *sagacity*!").

The aspect of the Apologies I hate the most is this: I am not a wise man, I am not an angry man, I am not a holy man. Yet the act of offering such self-conscious humility makes it seem as if I must be all of these— or at least must *believe* myself to be.

I want to say: I am a fourteen-year-old boy. I am still your son. You are the leaders here. I am happy with that.

Instead, I frown, try to look disapproving but gracious, try to look as if I appreciate the love that *must* be somewhere at the bottom of all this.

< 75 >

ELEVEN

IN COMIC BOOK SHOPS one often over-
hears conversations between obsessed,
chatty collectors and the persons who sit,
always looking very bored, behind the
counters. The boredom comes from the
condition of knowing everything. Obsessed, chatty collectors cannot resist the
hope of telling these persons something
they do not yet know, nor can they resist
the chance to bounce their own erudition
off a brighter surface.

One day I was browsing through a

< 76 >

shelf of used graphic novels, and I heard a talksy type—overanimated, full of blurt, incapable of listening—reveal that he had recently purchased an original sketch by Drake Jones at an auction.

I snuck a look. The longhaired teenager behind the counter almost lifted an eyebrow, which meant he was colossally intrigued. Encouraged, the collector (a middle-aged fat man with a beard trimmed to a thin line around his jaw and above his lips) went on to describe his emotions once he had gained possession of his treasure.

He said one very interesting thing. He said, "You know, having just one single, small piece of Drake's creation makes you feel like you possess it all. . . ."

< 77 >

TWELVE

I FELT MANY THINGS when my parents came back calling themselves newborn Christians. There was a lot to talk about. I wondered about how they had come to discover God, Jesus, etc. I wondered about what they had learned about the designing, and how they had learned it so fast. I wondered about what the specific policies of their sect might be.

I wanted the pleasure of talking with two smart people I loved about everything I could talk about with no one else.

< 78 >

At first I asked a few questions about the mechanics of their conversion. My parents answered them—politely but with some discomfort and restraint that surprised me. I expected to see more excitement, joy. Finding God is a pretty big deal. One naturally feels celebratory, expansive.

It occurred to me that perhaps they felt my inquiry might be a bit skeptical, even disapproving—as if I might consider myself the family authority on Jesus and religion. It also struck me that because I had suffered skepticism at their hands for years, they might fear a reprisal from me.

I stopped inquiring.

But I bided my time, and hoped to pick up clues from the conversations, rituals, and relationships that were certain to develop in the practice of their new faith.

This proved to be difficult, at least at first. My parents tended to talk earnestly to each other in low voices, and to trail off when I came upon them. It is true they prayed with great vigor and demonstrative joy, but these proclamations were so stylized they seemed impersonal, almost as if

< 79 >

the purpose of the noisiness was to obscure what was going on at a deeper level. The privacy was fine with me— Jesus is pretty clear on the issue of keeping your inner relationship with God inner. But the whoop-dee-doo stuff made me feel a bit toyed with.

Faith of Faiths appeared not to be a church-centered sect. Its followers were allowed to exercise their faith at home. Still, it seemed that *some* "fellowship" was encouraged, because my parents began to receive visits from two couples new to their acquaintance (and mine).

Neither of the couples seemed likely to have become friends of my parents without the link of Faith of Faiths. William and Ellen Erskine were thin, pale, erect people who never smiled with their lips parted, always dressed in ill-fitting dark-brown suits (he with a black knit tie, she with a white-collared blouse buttoned all the way up), and spoke with a lesson-teaching tone that seemed condescending, and often mildly scolding. It was clear that they were longtime members of the faith, who

< 80 >

called at our home every couple of weeks to monitor my parents' growth. They drank only hot water out of a steel thermos they brought with them (Mrs. Erskine carried it on a black woven strap over her shoulder like a small rifle), and ate only grapes and crackers. Their visits lasted an hour each, and consisted of reports from my father (on perceptions of a holy nature that led to revisions of lifestyle) to which Mr. Erksine responded with critiques and hints. The women never spoke.

I met the Erskines during their second visit. They both looked me over quickly but thoroughly, nodding to acknowledge my "Pleased to meet you." Then Mr. Erskine treated me to one of his lip-smiles and said, "Christ find you," and I was dismissed. Later, using the encounter as an excuse to probe a little, I asked my father what the Erskines did. "Hide from the sun, mostly," my mother said before she could stop herself. My father gave her an absolutely ferocious glare, and she flushed deeply and left the room with an apology. My father then turned to me and said,

< 81 >

"William is a seller of seeds."

"You mean like Burpee seeds? Or grain? Farm stuff?"

"Seeds that grow," my father said, and that was all I got.

Before their conversion, the friends who called on my parents had all been brilliant chattery types whose idea of a frolic was to drink fifty-dollar bottles of wine and argue about proposed immigration policies in the Southwest or the relative sappiness of Stevie Wonder's lyrics versus those of the Eagles. Their best buddies had been a couple named Maria Batistuta and Pete Ridley who had been married the same weekend as my parents; they all met on their honeymoons in Switzerland (and returned there together to ski for a week every February). Maria, who owned a huge *estancia* in Argentina, was a local public defender; Pete was a self-employed software genius who worked out of his home (he grew up in this city) inventing a new wizard program every other month or so. I used to hang around the edges of the evenings when

< 82 >

they came over, because they were terrific fun to be around, as were my parents in their company, at least until the marijuana or Halcion came out, at which point I always left.

The Batistuta-Ridleys did not appear for three weeks after my parents got back from Jamaica. This was an unusually long time for them to stay away. Then one night they showed up at the door, clutching a jeroboam of champagne and a new Bob Dylan CD, laughing, hugging, slapping backs. My parents responded to the bonhomie with chilly smiles and stiff backs and nervous glances. They did not touch the champagne, which Maria and Pete ended up drinking right out of the bottle when my mother pointedly failed to bring glasses. My father would not touch the Dylan CD himself, though he did not stop Pete when he insisted on putting it on the stereo. The nasal singer (for whom I am named) provided a weird, gloomy background to the strain of the night.

Throughout the evening, as their guests tried one desperate stratagem of

< 83 >

friendliness after another, my parents kept glancing at the door, looking as if they expected the Erskines might show up any minute and turn them into serpents. Maria and Pete began to look at the door, too. Finally, after firing off all their good-will and calling futilely upon all their historic references of intimacy, they stood up unsteadily and tried to hug my parents good-bye. Then they made their way to the foyer.

My parents remained standing in the living room. I walked their pals to the door.

Maria was weeping by the time she had her coat on. Pete gripped my arm and focused his eyes into mine.

"Zim, old buddy in Christ, this isn't *your* doing, is it?"

"No," I said. "They got this way on their vacation."

"Didn't call, see. Been back, what, three weeks? Never called. Maria said wait, they're jet-lagged, sunburned, hungover, whatever. Right, Maria?" Maria snurfed and muttered something in Spanish.

< 84 >

"What I wonder," said Pete, "is, like, is this *it*? *Finito*? I mean, is this *them*, now? And are we, like, Mr. and Mrs. Black Inverted Crucifix Dripping with Bat Blood? Don't darken the door again, that sort of deal?"

"I don't know," I said. "I really don't."

Pete peered at me, squeezed my arm. "How about you, Zimbo?"

"I never thought you were especially evil, Pete."

"Not what I mean," he said, shaking his head. "Not *us* evil. What about *you*? Do they think, you know, that *you* are deluded and wicked now too?"

"I'm not sure," I said. Maria had stopped crying and was listening now, with a sober frown. "I don't think so."

"Pretty hard switcheroo *that* would be," Pete said. "Go from being the weirdo prude to being the sinful knave in one week." He leaned forward and kissed me beneath my left eye. "Call if we can do anything. Or call if you want some sinful context, you want to be the weirdo prude again, hang out with some *real* nasties. We're always

< 85 >

glad." He had begun to cry now.

Maria kissed me—neatly on the lips—and they left.

The other couple who visited my parents was named McCorty. I never learned their first names. The first time they came, I happened to be passing through the living room as they stepped in; a short beefy man with a pink scalp and water-blue eyes bounded toward me with both arms outstretched. "McCorty!" he said joyously. I looked past him at my parents, who were trying with tired eyes to smile. By then the man had grabbed me and given me a quick squeeze.

"McCorty here," he said, thumping his rounded chest. I smelled rum so strongly I thought perhaps he had dipped his necktie in a Planter's Punch.

"Hi," I managed to say. "I'm Zimmerman."

"The little lady," he said grandly, sweeping his arm at his beaming wife, who had short brown curly hair and was wearing a tiny brimless hat. She actually gave me a curtsy.

< 86 >

I bowed slightly. Then I left.

I soon saw that for my parents the meetings with the McCortys were different from those with the Erskines. The roles were reversed. The Erskines set themselves up as arbiters of correctness. With them, my parents behaved like hesitant neophytes of the faith. The McCortys, on the other hand, came to confess their constant failure to hold to their new purity. My parents accepted these confessions grimly with a confident authority they showed toward no one else. Mr. McCorty drank a lot, coveted the young women in his office, stole money from his wife to buy drink and (of all things) old tools from antique stores (I gather he collected them with uncontrolled passion); Mrs. McCorty gambled at pinochle with her old friends, and routinely cheated them—an innovation *since* her conversion.

The McCortys seemed relieved and delighted to detail their sins; my parents seemed just as pleased to issue stern admonitions mixed with sympathetic nods.

< 87 >

Listening on the stairs, I wondered: Had someone—a leader in Faith of Faiths—set all of this up?

What a great idea! Allow your recruits to feel inferior to uptight scolds of greater piety, then superior to looser classmates of jolly temperament and weak will. Was there a pair of ice-people in front of whom the Erskines stammered and blushed? Was there a duo of slobs upon whom the McCortys frowned in righteousness? Why not?

< 88 >

THIRTEEN

MASON FARWELL IS the only shop-keeper on Main Street who does not follow an exact routine. The plastic clock with the movable hands behind the glass of his door always indicates that he *"Will Return At"* *10:00*, but in the past three weeks he has never arrived earlier than 10:22. There is one consistency: His is always the last business to open every day.

And once he is inside, he does not enact a repeated routine that precedes the opening of the shop, either. One morning

< 89 >

he took only eleven minutes to open the door, another morning he took thirty-four. His activities can be clearly observed through the windows. He drinks what looks like coffee with cream from a blue chipped mug bearing a white New York Yankees logo; he reads a newspaper; he scribbles numbers on a notepad; he makes telephone calls (one morning he made twelve); he examines some of the store's more valuable cards, with apparent curiosity; he eats donuts (brought in a garish pink-and-white-striped bag from a fast-food chain restaurant outside town, never bought fresh from his neighbor Jack Waller); he very frequently picks his nose and examines the discoveries on his fingertip before wiping them beneath the seat of his stool; he wanders around the store talking to himself, with gestures; he fiddles with the dial of a radio. Most of these things he continues to do after he has opened the shop, in addition to which he also rings up sales on his electronic cash register, puts merchandise into brown

< 90 >

paper bags, refills countertop display boxes.

Only on Saturdays is Mason Farwell joined in the shop by his partner, Allen Thomassen.

Saturday is the busiest day for Kollektible Kards. Boys are not at school, young men are not in the office; allowances and paychecks yearn to be spent. On Saturday Mr. Thomassen opens the shop precisely at 9:30. Mr. Farwell arrives around his usual time. And as if he does not notice the clamoring nine-year-olds hollering for price-guide quotations and the edgy yuppies trying to haggle five dollars from the price of a John Elway Topps rookie card, Mr. Farwell proceeds just as he always does, sipping coffee and reading the newspaper and jotting figures on a scratch pad.

Mr. Thomassen, however, works quite dynamically for the entire period he is in the store. He addresses all customers cheerily (most of them by name); calls out information about particular cards or sets

< 91 >

or price-guide valuation changes to people bending over glass cases, usually without being asked; straightens countertop displays, refilling boxes after every purchase; answers the telephone with brio, dispensing detailed information on the shop's inventory; and watches the Rack of Stars.

The Rack of Stars appears to be the province of Mr. Thomassen alone. With the exception of those weekday mornings when he picks up the valuable cards and studies them incredulously, I have never seen Mr. Farwell even glance at the Rack of Stars. It is Mr. Thomassen who selects the cards that will grace the Rack, a process of deliberation he performs with picturesque consideration (stroking his chin, saying "Let's see . . ." etc.) first thing every Saturday morning. It is he who converses with customers examining the cards displayed on the Rack, excitedly annotating the selections with every kind of anecdote and statistic. Finally, it is he, Mr. Thomassen, Saturdays only, who never quite takes his eyes off the Rack of Stars, especially when boys are in its vicinity.

< 92 >

During the week Mr. Thomassen works as a chemistry teacher at the high school. But it is obvious that he is at heart a devoted card collector (just as it is obvious Mr. Farwell is not). Mr. Thomassen's enthusiasm for discussing every nuance of card beauty, condition, and value; his broad grasp of the field's trends and ability to predict changes; his fussiness with the shop's merchandise—these things testify to the fact that he is part owner of the store simply so that he can acquire and show off a large number of terrific cards. Even though he must sell them (often with visible regret), it is plain that he feels these cards are *his*. And the Rack of Stars is his special, personal showcase.

Collectors who know Mr. Thomassen, or know the field, are aware that the "Stars" on the titled rack are not the athletes or superheroes pictured on the cardboard. No—the "Stars" are the cards *themselves*, as collectible items.

Thus a Kalawi Dupree gold-foil-imprinted Fleer rookie card is on the Rack, while similar editions of Marshall Faulk

< 93 >

and Drew Bledsoe lie in the ghetto of the glass cases, though Kalawi Dupree was a mediocre offensive lineman for a terrible team for two years before gaining too much weight and blowing out his left knee, never to play again. How then is this card worthy? Well, it so happens that on the day his rookie card was being printed (and a select number were being foil-embossed), the print run was shortened by a power outage at the Connecticut plant contracted by the Fleer company. Production for that day was cut by four fifths; the card most abbreviated was the Dupree. Its gilded version is especially hard to find. Mr. Thomassen acquired his at a card show in southern Ohio. He will sell it now for $1,800.

Other cards on the Rack sell for higher sums; the top card costs $10,000.

Shouldn't such cards be locked away? Shouldn't they be visible only through glass? One might expect to be able to handle them only by appointment, one on one with Mr. Thomassen.

But no. The Star cards sit on a special

< 94 >

golden rack (designed, built, and actually covered in gold leaf by Mr. Thomassen), in simple plastic cases only three eighths of an inch larger than the cards' borders— loose, unlocked. Vulnerable. Perhaps that is the point: Something about their vulnerability makes the act of displaying them more personal, to Mr. Thomassen. More honest, more collectorish, more we're-all-boys.

An item worth $10,000. Sized to slip into any shirt or jacket pocket. Right out on a rack that is watched carefully only one day a week.

It really is remarkable.

< 95 >

FOURTEEN

MY SON, WE HAVE much to be sorry for. . . ."

So far the Apologies have all been for small actions easily linked to explicit commandments made by Jesus, God, Moses, etc., in the Bible, and clearly transgressed in the instance cited. It is a pretty unimaginative reckoning. Perhaps it will grow more adventurous as the litany continues and the easier "sins" are accounted for.

At the moment, however, my father

< 96 >

has not mentioned some of the more interesting ways in which he and my mother
tried to pulverize my holy precedence.
There was the time when they put grain
alcohol—only a little, I admit—in my
Gatorade after a long bike ride my father
and I took together, just a joke to get me to
"loosen up" a bit, which they insisted I had
"earned" the right to do because I had rid-
den so far, so well. And there was the night
when, after I had refused a dozen invitations and cajolings to join a party in the
living room, they watched and protested
only between laughs as three of their
friends—two lawyers and a councilwoman—tried to hold me and stick one of
their little ivory hash pipes into my
mouth. I ended up cracking the mouth-
piece with my molars ("Hey, I brought
that pipe back from Kashmir!" pouted the
councilwoman).

My parents apologized abjectly a couple of hours later in my room, it is true
(and they never had those friends over to
the house again). Sitting on the edge of my

< 97 >

bed, my mother cried as if she had broken a bone. My father kept stroking my hair back off my forehead and saying, "We're just afraid you're going away and we want to keep you with us" and "We just want to bring you more into our life" and "We only want to share." I told him I had gone nowhere; it was he who was letting stupid drugs run away somewhere with *his* head; perhaps he ought to see that I already *was* in his life, and that the only thing he could do was drive me *out*; maybe he shouldn't try to share destruction with someone he supposedly loved.

"Don't judge us, Zimmerman," my mother snurfed.

"I think you've got it backward," I said. "It's you who judge me. It's you who decide I need 'loosening up' and 'heightened liveliness' and 'a touch of sophistication' and all that trash." I snorted. "What's next? Is Dad going to take me to a whore and buy me half an hour?"

"Please don't be vulgar," she said. "We are trying to accept you."

"You've already accepted me," I said.

< 98 >

"You accepted me the day I was born. This is something else."

My mother, crying, tried to protest, but my father, looking interested, said, "What is it? What do you think?"

I was angry. "Beats me," I said. "I'm not the one who's had a son for fourteen years."

I sniffed. My father, looking as if he had been stricken with malaria, stroked my hair with a hand that shook. My mother took a deep breath.

"It's just love," she said.

"Oh," I said. "Well, in *that* case . . ."

"Don't laugh," she said. "It is. It's love. That's all we feel for you: nothing but love."

My dad, his voice quivering a little, said, "I think maybe we feel something else."

My mother snapped him a look. "What?" I asked.

He shrugged, and sighed, and pulled his hand away. "We want to be loved back."

I gaped. "You think I don't love you?"

"We want to be loved more than God,"

< 99 >

he said, looking at my bedspread. After a moment, he looked up sideways at my mother, who was staring at him. "We want a demonstration. Small of us, I guess. In fact, I'm sure. But that's it, isn't it?" he asked.

She tried to nod. I could tell. But she couldn't do it. He waited for a long time, watching her. Finally, she gave a single shake of her head, and looked down.

The most serious of their encouragements to get loose took place one night as we sat peacefully in the living room after dinner. My father sat in his leather chair doing a British crossword puzzle; my mother sat on the Kashmiri rug in a full lotus (excellent for the spine) reading three newspapers spread around her; I sat on the edge of the Italian wool sofa doing my algebra homework at the walnut coffee table. From the FM radio came mellow white swing jazz from the 1930s, digitally remastered and broadcast in simulated stereo.

My mother suddenly looked up with a perky expression. "Zim, my sweet," she said.

< 100 >

"Yes?"

She glanced down and smoothed an item in one of her newspapers. "Wasn't there some comic-book genius you were obsessed with at one time? Some prodigy or something who started this whole kind of publishing all by himself?"

I stopped writing a quadratic equation. "Yes," I said. "His name is Drake Jones."

She nodded and took a sip of Cabernet, squinting at the page (she needed glasses but refused to get them until she turned forty). "And are you still interested in his stuff?"

"Probably," I said, putting my pencil down. "What kind of 'stuff'?"

She tapped the paper. "Some kind of card or something, like a baseball card, or something." She squinted closer. "Pretty valuable?"

I shrugged. "If it's from one of the bootleg copies of his original series, it's probably worth fifty dollars or so."

"And if it's one of the original cards themselves?"

I got up went over to where she sat,

< 101 >

kneeling and looking at the paper she had been pointing to. There was a six-inch story in the middle of the page, beneath a photo of two men standing in front of a rack of small cards in a store. The headline said NEW VENTURE HOPES FOR YOUTHFUL PATRONS. "That's very doubtful," I said.

"How much?" she persisted, as I scanned.

"I don't know," I said, "at least a thousand dollars or so."

She whistled.

The article described the conversion of a fuddy-duddy old stamp-and-coin store into a laser-fresh cards-and-comics marketplace.

I saw Drake Jones's name and focused on it.

The passage read:

> In addition, every week special cards will be featured as marquee items that the owners hope will "show we have the class items to play with the big boys," laughs Thomassen.

< 102 >

Rookie cards of great sports stars (Nolan Ryan, Drew Bledsoe, Shaquille O'Neal), music nostalgia cards (The Beatles, Elvis Presley), and cards of comic book heroes (from Marvel, Image, Drake Jones) can be studied with longing—or even taken home, for anywhere between $300 and $10,000!

"Interesting," I said, getting back up. I glanced at my mother. She was watching me with a kind of crafty amusement that I was used to seeing only in advance of an idea I would not like.

"Wait," she said. "Look at the picture."

I glanced down, then back at her. "I saw it."

"*What* did you see?"

"Two old guys smiling for the camera in their new store with the fruity name."

She shook her head with amused patience and took another sip of wine. From the corner of my eye I saw my father lower his crossword and watch us over his glasses.

"You're missing it," my mother said.

< 103 >

I fought back a sigh of exasperation. "Why don't you just tell me."

She looked over at my father. He took his glasses off, crossed his knees, and leaned forward.

"Am I correct in assuming you would like to own one of these Drake Jones cards? I mean, aside from their monetary worth, which I am sure is beneath your lofty consideration, are they intrinsically valuable items of interest?"

"I've never even seen one," I said.

"Well, how would you like to see one every day, in the privacy of your own room?"

I looked at both of them. "I don't understand—is this a pre-Christmas shopping investigation or something? Are you looking for gift ideas? If so, I'd rather—"

"I'm thinking of you giving a gift to yourself," she said, nodding and bouncing with a mild glee. Her cheeks were flushed from the wine and her idea. "*Two* gifts," she laughed, with a quick look at my father. "One of which is liberty."

The word "liberty" spoken by my

< 104 >

mother to me always meant doing some-thing wild that would break the self-imposed bondage of my moral rectitude. I ignored this and pretended to take her lit-erally. "If it's a matter of liberty," I said, "I choose freely not to spend fifty bucks on a card, even as a 'gift' to myself."

"Save your money," she said, eyes sparkling. "But have the card." A pause; then, leaning forward, *"Have the card,* Zimmerman."

Across the room my father got it, and nodded with a chuckle.

I sighed. "All right," I said. "I'm not hip enough to get all of these oblique hints. What are you talking about, Mom?"

She took a sip, smiled at me, chose her words. "I'm talking," she said, in a calmer voice, "about a little initiative. A little dar-ing." She watched me. "A little act of— *Revolution.* Christ was kind of a revolution-ary, wasn't he?"

"So was Hitler."

"Take the plunge," my father said.

"Take the *card,*" my mother said.

And suddenly I got it. I understood.

< 105 >

I saw her point, comprehended her glee. For a moment I could do nothing but stand and stare at her. Then I was able to say, in a voice much slower and more controlled than my heartbeat, "You are suggesting that I steal something."

She laughed. My father said, "I always knew you were a bright boy."

"But it's not as nasty as you make it sound, now, Zimmerman," my mother said quickly.

"Theft?" I said, letting my incredulity begin to show. "Not nasty? That's not what you thought when someone looted the stereo and computers while we were in Maine last summer."

"That was personal," said my father.

"Aren't those persons?" I said, pointing to the photo of the two men.

"Not really," my mother said. "They now represent a kind of exploitative commerce that imposes artificial valuation that stands between you and a simple, almost worthless item you wish in all innocence to possess."

"Wow, Comrade, from your advertising

< 106 >

business I would never have suspected you had such a keen grasp of capitalism's evils."

"Don't be disrespectful," warned my father.

"Disrespectful? You are encouraging your son to steal!"

My mother was shaking her head at both of us. Making a point of addressing my father—but really speaking to me—she brought the whole thing back to familiar ground: "Honey, you don't understand. Zim isn't being disrespectful to me. His problem, really, is being *too* respectful. . . ." And so on. Just another seminar on my neurotic and futile pursuit of some unattainable perfection that would make me feel holy. I relaxed; it was actually almost nice to hear the old words on the old theme. The further we got from the advocacy of theft the better.

I must have shown my relief a little too clearly, must have let my mother notice how my mind was wandering away from her lesson, because just as she was finishing up, she produced, as if from nowhere,

< 107 >

a zinger that darted through my day-dreaming.

"As for Zimmerman," she said, fixing me with a bright look that was more confident and expectant than hopeful, "I think we all should remember this: There may come a time when he wants to show us—and himself—that he's simply human, that he's not a saint, that he doesn't pretend to be." She paused, and smiled warmly. "Something impulsive, something *wrong*, like swiping a little card would do that. But we should give him time. Maybe he's not ready."

< 108 >

FIFTEEN

IT SEEMS THAT from the start, even before he had the help of the inkers and letterers who worked on his earliest underground comic books, Drake Jones had no trouble turning the strange images in his mind into strange images on paper.

For example, the trading card he drew of a superhero called Nightface demonstrates an ability to imply distances, atmosphere, and character, all in a strictly limited space.

The card features a figure high on a

< 109 >

dark rock outcropping, leaning to look down on a thin white path curving over a bald hill far below. On that path one can just see another figure, very small, hurrying away toward the vanishing point. One's first feeling is that this small figure must be in danger, probably from the larger presence looking down from the rock. But something is not right in this assumption. The rock on which the larger figure stands—obviously it is Nightface—is flat but severely tilted; this is no safe perch. In fact, the path below looks more secure. A visibly potent wind—seen in the way the small figure's cape whips out behind, and the way a scraggly tree behind Nightface twists and reaches—makes the hero's place seem more perilous still. His pointed cowl looks as if it were about to be ripped right back off his face.

Or—aha!—one should say, ripped right back off the face he would have beneath the cowl if in fact he had a face.

He does not.

Above the short stiff black collar of the usual skintight superhero body-stocking,

<110>

and below the folded edge of the cowl, right where all other superheroes have foreheads, brows, eyes glaring with intelligence or malice or beatitude, sharp noses, jutting chins—right there, in that space, Nightface has nothing but the night itself. The high darkness surrounding him on his precarious rock, the low darkness through which the path cuts down below—it seems to begin beneath that cowl, above that collar. I don't know how Drake did it, with a pretty simple drawing of a guy on a rock, but somehow he makes the night look as if it flows out of Nightface. And that seems perfectly natural.

Questions occur. One wants to ask them directly of this partial person, who, despite his oddity, seems somehow a figure of sadness, and, therefore, a figure one can meet. One wants to ask: What happened to you? What can you *do*, with the night for your face? What power has been given, or taken away?

Are you good?

If you are good, are you good in ways that mystify most people, the way the

< 111 >

strange comforts of the night do?

Are you alone?

Does no one understand?

It is a feature of all forty-four cards in Drake's series that each scene on the front is described briefly in words on the back, a strange doubling of imagery that may reveal a lot about Drake himself, actually— his layered perception, his sense of the equipoise between word and picture, his distrust of singular expression, his need to surround his reader without really defining anything. Or, perhaps, the twice-told aspect of his cards may simply reflect his budding printer's interest in typeface and design.

In any case, there is a boxed paragraph describing the scene. In addition, the back of the card contains a flush-right list of vital statistics about the depicted character: age, height, weight, life expectancy. Then, sometimes, there is a simple statement revealing an unexpected detail about the character's interior life.

Once, very briefly, this printed material from all forty-four cardbacks appeared

< 112 >

in a small book—a Ph.D. thesis, actually, written at the University of North Dakota and published by the university press. But Drake Jones filed an immediate lawsuit and publication was stopped through an injunction; supposedly, fewer than fifty copies of the book escaped into the world. I have never seen a copy.

The images on the fronts of the cards have never been reproduced.

Nightface is one of the characters who receives a statement of interior revelation. On the back of his card, in 6-point Typo Roman, Drake set the sentence:

NIGHTFACE SEEKS ASYLUM
IN THE HIGHEST OF PLACES

< 113 >

SIXTEEN

PERHAPS I COULD have watched forever in silence as my parents enjoyed their swings from inferiority to superiority, all in the spirit, apparently, of Christ. But after a few months, something changed in their relationships to both the Erskines and the McCortys. It was obvious that the change had something mysterious to do with me.

It began one night when the Erskines were there. I was upstairs in my room, reading a book for which a couple of schol-

< 114 >

ars had collected about forty wildly different documents all claiming to depict the true history of Jesus's lost years of youth. A knock came on my door.

It was my father. He smiled nervously and asked if I would join them downstairs.

As we walked into the room Mr. Erskine turned his eyes on me with a hungry look of curiosity. It was not a look really directed at me—I felt he was seeing someone else walking around with my face.

"Ah, my young gentleman," he said, rising and smiling more warmly than I had expected.

I mumbled something polite.

"Sit, please," Mr. Erskine said grandly, indicating a chair, as if this weren't my living room. I sat. He did too, never taking his eyes off me.

No one said anything for perhaps two minutes. Then Mr. Erskine nodded. "Thank you," he said to me.

"For what?" I said.

"For—why, for making yourself available." He nodded again.

< 115 >

I looked at my father. He looked back with a kind of pleading stillness, as if he were afraid of being shot if I showed a lack of grace. I shrugged to Mr. Erskine. "Well," I said, "sure."

That seemed to satisfy him. He sat back a bit, and began a very elementary and boring lecture on the importance of moderating free will. The lecture was directed at my parents. He never even glanced at me. When he finished, he nodded to his wife, and they got up and left. My parents barely caught them at the coat closet.

"Do they always leave like that?" I asked, when my father came back into the living room.

He nodded distractedly, then sat down. After a moment he looked up at me. "I hope you will join us," he said.

"You mean come down here and listen to that man's lectures once in a while? Or join you by joining your church?"

He blushed. "I would hope . . . I mean, it isn't necessary for you to . . . I don't think your mother and I would presume—"

< 116 >

"That's okay," I said. "As for these evenings, sure, I'll come down when you want me to. At least once in a while." I hesitated, and frowned. "But I can't promise to pay attention unless he gets more interesting."

"Thank you," my father said with a relief I did not understand.

The next time the McCortys came, much the same thing happened; Mr. McCorty surprised me with an avid, sober scrutiny that was almost a match for Mr. Erskine's. The next hour consisted of an unusually detailed exegesis of his fleshly sins. I sat through it, looking mostly at my feet.

My father continued to invite me down whenever the Erskines or McCortys came to call. Always, I was studied with obvious approval. Once in a while, my opinion on a matter of simple morality was requested by Mr. Erskine ("I wonder what our young man thinks about the matter of telling 'white lies' . . ."). Every session held no interest for me; these people did not discuss anything. I was there only

< 117 >

because my father seemed to want me to be present. I thought perhaps he wanted me to check out the goods—to form an educated opinion about the people he was joining. At the risk of sounding pompous, I thought he was depending on me to be his advisor, consultant, expert.

I could not have been more wrong.

< 118 >

S E V E N T E E N

THIS MORNING MR. FARWELL opens the store after only twelve minutes.

Nine minutes later, a middle-aged man in a tan raincoat walks through the front door. His name is McGregor, he is a salesman, he has been out of work for six months. He comes into the store every day at least three times, spending between $18 and $36 per visit. Possibly he is addicted to collecting sports and superhero cards. Because some very valuable cards are hidden randomly in certain kinds of packs,

< 119 >

for some people it is a form of gambling, and I believe this may be the case with Mr. McGregor; he usually takes his packs of cards in a small brown bag around the corner into the alley, where he opens them quickly and efficiently, one after the next, flipping with grim concentration through the cards in each pack, registering no joy or disappointment, even when he pulls a card that he then carefully slips into his breast pocket. Often, when he has put two or three cards into his breast pocket he goes back into the store and can be seen trading these apparently valuable cards in for more packs, which he then opens in the alley as before. On days when Mr. McGregor fails to find any cards worthy of his breast pocket, he drops his bag, his packet wrappers, his worthless cards, and his receipt onto the brick floor of the alley.

Six minutes later, while Mr. McGregor is still in the store, a teenage boy in a Devil Rays hooded jacket also enters. His name is Jervis. He is often suspended from the high school (for truancy), and on those days when he does not attend classes he

< 120 >

seems to start his day (and often end it) in Kollektible Kards. He rarely buys anything. To him the store appears to serve a function something between a library and a museum. He can be seen going out for coffee once in a while, for Mr. Farwell; these errands seem to earn him the right to linger in the shop without any pretense of becoming a cash customer.

Ten minutes after Jervis, I too go into Kollektible Kards.

Mr. Farwell is drinking coffee and grimacing at the newspaper's sports page as I enter. He does not even glance up.

Mr. McGregor stands three-quarters of the way toward the rear of the shop (which is fifty-one feet from front door to rear wall; it is also fourteen feet wide, with glass cases along the right-hand side, with an employees-only aisle running behind it, and bookcases holding various boxes of cards flush against the left-hand wall). Jervis is studying several pricey rookie cards of NBA players, on the Rack of Stars.

< 121 >

EIGHTEEN

I'M NOT CERTAIN when the Apologies began to change into excuses for praising me. I should have noticed right away and taken steps to head off this new trend, but I didn't spot the change because I had stopped listening to my father whenever he adopted that humble, worshipful tone.

At least I hope that is why I didn't spot the change. I hope it was just failure to notice, and not the fact that on some level I had noticed all too well and wished the praise to continue.

< 122 >

In any case, one day a few months ago the two of us were in the garage, cleaning up tools and workshop scraps. Scraping rust from a wrench handle, I suddenly went cold in a silence following something he had said a few seconds before.

"What did you say?" I asked.

He was using steel wool on the blade of a plane; he did not look up.

"Oh, just that a person of your sanctity, at such a young age, with such adherence to purity in the adversities you faced, must be marked by God for a holy purpose."

I grunted. "Then you said something else."

He focused intently on the plane. "Oh, just that, well, I think there must be a faith you could, well, sort of become a *model* for. A spokesman or something. A kind of inspiring figure who sort of embodies—"

"I believe you used the word 'saint,' did you not?"

He put down the plane, took a deep breath, and looked at me. "Yes," he said. "I did. What I said in fact was 'living saint.' It's, well, kind of a new idea—"

< 123 >

"Whose?"

"Excuse me?"

"Whose idea?"

He stared at me, and swallowed a couple of times. "In fact, it's something that came to The Pastor John, himself."

"Himself. You mean—"

"Kind of a *cognition*, is what he calls them. He receives these direct gifts from God, what some people used to call visions—"

"And one of them was about me?"

My father's eyes changed a little. "Not one!" he said, shaking his head and letting the hint of an eager smile show. "Many! Many of them! Many times now, God has sent cognitions of *you* to Luke Mark John! And Luke Mark John *calls* us—several times a week! *Us—this family!* Do you have any idea what a privilege that is?" Then he let his joy show, raising his fists and pouring love from his eyes at the son that had thus attracted the eye of his leader, and maybe even God.

"It is indeed," I said.

By now he could not contain himself.

< 124 >

He was off his stool and bounding all over the garage, gesturing with both hands as if practicing to preach a sermon on TV. *His* son! *This* family! In a few minutes it became clear that these "cognitions" had been going on for a long time, beginning soon after I had met the great man at the airport. It became clear, too, that the ideas had not taken long to form into a very worldly scheme.

I was supposed to become the poster boy for Faith of Faiths.

But an active poster boy: a speaker, a *proclaimer*, a saver of souls, a leader of youth. It seems that for quite a while The Pastor John had been concerned about his faith's failure to penetrate all the way into the families whose parents he had brought to salvation on the sparkling beaches. Too often, when they got home, they were unable to reach out to their lost teenagers: in fact, too often their own faith served merely to alienate the pitifully sinful youth even further. As a result, quite a few of the parents—being loving Christians— had been unable to resist the pull toward

< 125 >

their children, and had drifted away from old double-F.

The Erskines were such a couple—or they had nearly become one. However, instead of drifting away from their faith, the Erskines had held to it, as their fifteen-year-old son departed and went to live with a heavy-metal band that played benefits for abortion clinics. Thus, the Erskines were deemed particular experts about youth and the problem of reaching it.

The Erskines, after months of observation, agreed with The Pastor John about what was needed.

What was needed was a young champion to shine forth and dispel the gloom of ignorance that hung between the generations.

And lo, God had sent one. A strong, handsome pure lad—a "natural" follower of Christ, who had purified himself (at least up to the point where he needed to join Faith of Faiths for the final blessing), whose life was exemplary, who had resisted all the worldly temptations that sucked down his brothers and sisters in youth—and indeed,

< 126 >

their parents and grandparents too. Never had there been such a kid! He was truly a "living saint" and he could not fail to bring "millions" (or maybe even dozens) of lost teenagers to the glorious salvation of the Faith (of Faiths).

Somewhere in the middle of this my father began to weep with the bliss of it. I had never seen my father cry before; I had never seen him this happy. He kept talking, trying hard to sound practical, the way he knew I would like to hear such plans expressed, but he could not hide his pleasure. Indeed, I felt an ache, a sweet pain so deep it was as if I had a place in me I had never known of, and I reached out for him. He ran into my arms, sobbing and laughing, smacking my back with one hand as he squeezed me. He was proud, he said. So proud, at last. What a relief it was at last to love me for myself, he said. He had never loved me more.

< 127 >

N I N E T E E N

JERVIS HAS MOVED approximately eighteen feet away from the Rack of Stars to a glass case near the front.

Mr. McGregor still studies a card or cards in the glass case to the rear of the store, approximately twenty-five feet away.

Mr. Farwell turns a page, glances up as Jervis laughs, apparently at a price on a card in the case, and looks back down at his paper.

I walk calmly over to the Rack of Stars.

< 128 >

Marcos wrote: *In prison there is nothing else to do but worship God.*

Asylum means: a safe place to be. Especially when one is pressed.

< 129 >

TWENTY

WHENEVER I HAVE HEARD about an amazing prodigy in some field—the three-year-old chess wizard, the four-year-old physicist, the eight-year-old violinist—I have thought of Jesus.

Jesus was a prodigy, was he not? A typical prodigy. In the Bible, there are the stories of how, at a very young age, he amazed his elders with his grasp of scriptural matters. We never hear what happened to Jesus during the latter part of his childhood and his adolescence, but from

< 130 >

our experience with the weirdly blessed children of our time, we can imagine—that he was off somewhere confounding wise men in all parts of the known world. If Jesus had been a violinist, he would have been giving astonishing concerts in these places, scorching the air with his audacious flashes of genius, then disappearing into the night for the next town. If he had been a chess wizard, he would have checkmated the sage masters at each stop, after absorbing their historic strategies. A fast, romantic life, full of intensity, hunger, the need to make great things. A fierce adolescence.

As for adulthood—when he came home, he was misunderstood, hated, tortured, and murdered.

Drake Jones was certainly a prodigy. He saw things others did not, made great works, humiliated his elders, became rich in all worldly ways, but seemed only to care about unfolding new masterpieces. By the time he was twenty-one, Drake ruled a new world of his own making.

As for adulthood—before *he* could be

< 131 >

misunderstood, hated, tortured, possibly even murdered, Drake Jones disappeared. Like Jesus, he left a body of knowledge that continued to expand; and like Jesus, Drake himself continued to send new works from afar (four new comics in his hand have been launched since he vanished, and two extinct strips cunningly revived). Finally, like Jesus, Drake disappeared to join his father: In a statement printed in each of his comics announcing his "withdrawal," Drake explained that he was not going off alone—his dad was coming too.

There is a lot of guessing, of course, about where Drake and his father have gone. There are even magazines—two of them, published in alternate months—devoted entirely to "drakehunting." Mostly they print rumors, eyewitness accounts of "sightings," detailed analytical speculations, open letters from fans pleading with Drake to emerge from hiding, etc. Last year, one of the 'zines organized a three-week summer bus tour to visit twelve of the rumored hot spots; a travelogue of the

< 132 >

group's junket filled the next issue and showed that everyone had a wonderful time. Drake was never spotted, but that did not seem to matter.

< 133 >

through which filled the trail he saw what showed that someone had in truth left their shelter in very recent . . . but did not seem important.

TWENTY-ONE

Every weekday morning Mr. Farwell receives a telephone call at exactly 11:10.

It is 11:08 now. Jervis chuckles at his case of cards. McGregor frets at his.

Mr. Farwell has looked up and seen me at the Rack of Stars, however briefly.

The phone call will last less than two minutes.

I glance confidently along the top row of the Rack, running my eye left to right.

It is not there anymore.

With a freeze of panic I run my eye right

< 134 >

to left, and then back a third time, past the faces of baseball players, basketball rookies, football goons. It is gone.

With an involuntary gasp, perhaps even a small cry, I spin toward Mr. Farwell. I have opened my mouth to ask him, to accuse him of selling it, to wail at my failure, the consequences of which spin and peck along the outer edges of my shock. But before I can speak the phone rings. He answers it.

Delayed, furious, mouth moving, I turn back to the Rack, my eyes roving without intention or hope. And there, in the third row from the top, is the card.

There is Nightface.

My hand shakes as I reach out and touch the case, pick it up, hold it in the light coming in from the front window.

< 135 >

TWENTY-TWO

IN THE WEEKS following our revelatory hour in the garage, my father did not mention the scheme to make me the salvation of world youth. Nor did he return to the personal elation the scheme had brought forth in him. Instead, he resumed the process of making an Apology at least once a day.

The Apologies continued to ripen into sessions of Praise, incrementally, as if they were carefully planned to build up my tolerance for being adored.

< 136 >

Then, three weeks ago, our dinner was interrupted by the telephone. When my father returned to the table, he was pink with emotion and his hand shook as he picked up his goblet of mineral water and drank it down.

He looked at my mother, eyes flaring. She read his eyes for a moment, then turned pale except for two red spots on her cheekbones. She put her fork down.

They both looked at me.

My father cleared his throat. "That was The Pastor John," he said.

A small whimper escaped my mother.

I said nothing.

"He—he is going to come and pay us a visit," my father said, glancing at my mother. She put her napkin up to her mouth with both hands and kept it there.

"In three weeks," my father said. He looked back at me. He was very nervous. He tried a smile. "Actually, Son, he wants—it's *you* he wants to see."

"Ah," I said.

"He wants to spend a little time with you."

< 137 >

This time it was my mother's joy that popped the cork first. "Oh, Zimmerman," she gushed, tears starting, "we are so proud, so happy—"

But it was the wrong moment and my father cut her off with a chopping gesture. She gulped her way back to being quiet, but a tear snaked down each cheek. My father said, "The Pastor John asked—he does not know of our talk a few weeks ago—he asked that I—"

"He wants to spring the whole thing on me himself, but he wants you to have me"—I smiled briefly, in spite of myself, as the words came back—"softened up."

"Well," said my father, still nervous but sensing the chance for relief, "yes."

I nodded.

My father went on. "When he arrives, he wants me to tell him—to be able to tell him—that you are, well, um, probably ready to, um, receive a kind of special blessing—"

"Dad—"

"Of course, of course," he said, holding up his shaking palms, retreating, "of

< 138 >

course I don't expect you to promise me anything, not *now* or anything. . . . I mean, of course I, we, hope, just hope you see the . . . the *honor—*"

"Oh but, dear, he *will* accept," said my mother, looking at my father. "Zimmerman just needs to be ready, that's all." She looked at me. No tears now, just will. "Zimmerman will make himself ready, all by himself."

My father nodded. "Sure," he said. "I just hope he knows—"

"He knows," said my mother, still looking at me. Her smile widened. "He knows, that we love him, that we love Jesus, and that there is simply no way he can refuse."

< 139 >

TWENTY-THREE

THE PRICES OF collectible cards are often cited to exemplify how silly our consumer culture has become ("Two thousand dollars for a baseball card!"). But in fact the card market is a pure example of the responsive economy of supply and demand, in which something of no inherent value acquires only the worth placed on it by that great repository of wisdom, The People. The owner of a card store puts a tag of $2,000 on a Topps rookie card of Nolan Ryan. If someone comes in the next day and buys

< 140 >

it, the owner prices his next Ryan rookie card at $2,075. If that one sells in three days, his next will cost $2,150. If it sits for two months, he knows he has gone too high, and the price drops back to $2,075. If it sits two months longer, he concludes interest has slackened in Nolan Ryan, and hopes he won't have to go below $1,750 to sell his six remaining Ryan rookies.

If people won't pay it, the price drops. The customer decides.

A price of $10,000 for an original Drake Jones Nightface card actually strikes me as just. There is no sense of money when it comes to something so great; ten times the amount would still seem reasonable.

I feel certain no one would agree with me.

I can hear the incredulity now: "A card of a guy with no face? Ten thousand tacos?"

It is just a piece of cardboard.

Mr. Thomassen has put a ridiculous price on it because he likes having such an expensive item out in the open—possession as an act of daring.

< 141 >

But what of the risk to the card itself? I almost say: to Nightface himself? Doesn't someone whose quest is for asylum deserve a chance to find it, instead of representing an audacious dare?

The "price" is no true price at all. It is a mere artifice of (essentially deceitful) public relations, like the "New! Richer Flavor!" claim emblazoned across a box of breakfast cereal. So the theft of such an item could not reasonably be construed as truly "grand" larceny.

I think of these things as I hold the item itself, in the light coming through the shop's front window.

It strikes me that I have heard someone else say things very similar—things with which I disagreed. Thinking back, I recall that it was my mother.

I recognize that her angle on the matter then, and my angle now, are exactly opposite.

For a moment, I wonder if that makes any difference.

< 142 >

TWENTY-FOUR

BEFORE JAMAICA, the closest my parents came to religion—or acknowledging what I call the design of things—came during a period in which they strained to get as close as possible to the interior of natural systems and settings. Their inquiry manifested as a desire to get physically involved with such places as forests and canyons, so there were many rafting expeditions in rushing rivers, canoe trips to slice through silent waters, camping treks to sleep among huge trees and rocks.

< 143 >

Every weekend, and every vacation, took us "deep into the secrets of things," as my mother liked to say.

This happened only a year or so after I "got all Goddish" (my mother again). I recall a camping trip, when I acted as if I, by dint of my superior insight, had been appointed Guide to Enlightened Appreciation of Nature's Subtle Mechanics. As we hiked through a spruce forest, I explained what it meant to be evergreen. As we passed through a meadow of wildflowers, I made my parents stop several times— wobbling with their heavy backpacks—to observe particular plants that gave me the chance to lecture on photosynthesis and pollination. When we finally arrived at a beautiful dale near a tumbling stream, I explained the seasonal nature of a river's flow.

They listened to every word attentively.

What a task.

It went on all weekend. I never stopped. My parents just kept smiling, nodding, saying "Oh, yes?" and "Hmm, really?" and "Wow." Then, on the last

< 144 >

evening, as my father and I fished quietly from a dinghy in the middle of a small pond, I began to tell him about how fish used their gills. Nodding and murmuring as he had for three days, my father put his rod down, gently reached across and took mine from my hands, and, saying "Is that so?" calmly flung the whole rig in a cartwheel through the evening air. It landed with a surprisingly small splash over near some cattails, and sank.

I sputtered, "What did you do?"

He reached over and took me softly by the arms and slid me along my seat until I was close to him. Then he put his arms around me and pulled me against his chest.

"What are you doing?" I repeated.

"Don't know, do you?" he said, rocking me gently.

"No. I don't understand—that was a very good—"

"Just shut up, then."

"What?"

"Be quiet. That's what people do when they don't know what's going on. When

< 145 >

they don't understand. They shut up."

I shut up for a minute. He held me. I breathed in the scent of old bass scales from his vest, and watched sideways as some swallows began to wheel and dip over the pond's placid face.

In a softer voice, I said, "Were you just trying to do something I could not explain? Is that why you threw my pole away?"

"You got it," he said. He chuckled. "It's actually hard. To find something. You understand so much. But it's okay to be a little mystified sometimes."

I let him rock me. I opened one eye and watched the swallows. Each one eats about four thousand insects a day. You can know that, and still be mystified. Still.

< 146 >

TWENTY-FIVE

LAST NIGHT I CAME downstairs to drink a glass of milk before going to bed and found my parents in the living room with another person. It was Luke Mark John, wearing an old red wool letter jacket with black leather sleeves and a plain navy blue baseball cap. On the floor beside him was a heavy canvas Gladstone with leather and brass fittings.

The three of them turned and watched me as I walked across the rug to them; but almost immediately my parents switched

< 147 >

their eyes back, to observe their leader as he continued to look at me.

He smiled, and put out his hands as before. This time I extended my right hand only, in the traditional handshake fashion, and after a moment of hesitation and an amused flicker in his eyes, he took it in both of his. "The son," he said.

"At least, *a* son," I said. I nodded toward my parents. "Theirs."

His eyes sparked. "We are all sons of God," he said.

"Then we are all equal," I said. "Nothing special about being a son at all."

He laughed. After a moment of horrified uncertainty, my parents tried to chuckle along with him. He glanced at them, and back at me.

"Is this spontaneous humility?" he said, shaking my hand again. "Or do I suspect you've had some prologue to my visit and its purpose?"

"Your suspicions are known only to you," I said, "but I should absolve my father: I am a real weasel for information, and I construct nutty ideas from the scantiest data."

< 148 >

He broke into a genuine merry laugh, released my hand, and lightly punched my right biceps with his left hand. "The implication being, of course, that I construct the same sort of things?"

I shrugged. "If you have that sort of data."

He laughed hard. It was the best laughing I had heard for a long time. It was difficult not to like him.

My parents stood and watched us, hesitating to do anything. The Pastor John's laugh wound down into an "Ohhh my." He scratched his beard, glanced again at my parents, and cocked an eyebrow back at me.

"You are a good young man," he said. "Maybe even the best I have ever met."

"Perhaps you don't know me well enough."

He shook his head. "You'd be surprised how fast I can know such things. And besides—I have heard confirmation from many who have spent more time around you."

"The ever-acute Erskines."

< 149 >

He shrugged. "Perhaps the Erskines are not the *perfect* people to see deep into your soul. But there are others, not least these people here." He raised his hand toward my parents, without looking at them.

"They kind of *have* to like me."

He chuckled. "Well, then, I can tell you, most parents of fourteen-year-old boys don't do what they *have* to. No—I can know about you all by myself. I felt your goodness before we even met, and when I *did* touch your hand and see your eyes, it was clear you were special." He gave me a Serious Probing Look, then mocked it with a wink. "There is simply nothing bad about you, Zimmerman. You do nothing bad."

"Perhaps I simply haven't done it yet."

He laughed again. This one ended quickly, though, and he looked at me seriously, without the wink. "Then you'd better hurry. Tomorrow, at noon, if you will be so kind as to listen to me, I hope to offer you the chance to celebrate your goodness by dedicating it to God." He peered at his

< 150 >

watch with humorous exaggeration. "That gives you only thirteen hours." He tapped me on the shoulder and nodded. "Go to sleep, my boy, and say your prayers in the morning. Tomorrow," he said, smiling for the first time directly to my parents, "his life changes forever."

< 151 >

TWENTY-SIX

NIGHTFACE, IRONICALLY, is beautiful in the light of day.

Holding the card up in my right hand, still looking at it, I turn so that I am almost facing the front of the store. Beyond the card I can plainly see Mr. Farwell, head down, listening to his phone call. There may be only a few seconds more.

With my left hand I undo the button of my wool pea jacket. Its heavy lapels swing apart and hang open, its wide inner

< 152 >

pocket gaping. It is not a high place, but it is a place.

Mr. Farwell is nodding. He usually does that just before hanging up. My heart, which I expected to be pounding, beats coolly, lightly.

It is nearly time.

My mother, oddly, was right, though perhaps she wouldn't feel the same way now.

She said: There would be a time when I was ready.

She said: They only had to wait.

She said: A time would come, when I would see that there was simply nothing else I could do.

Mr. Farwell hangs up. Seeing some motion from my direction, he glances at me.

Asylum.

"Hey," he says, struggling quickly off his stool. "What the hell—"

< 153 >

The only thing wrong with his story—
the only part that didn't tug at her
heart—was the part about being royal.

If he had come along, telling her he had evidence
of her biological family and that they lived in
Cleveland, she would have been thrilled. But this
business of royalty tipped the story into the realm
of fairy tale, making it something she couldn't
entirely believe.

Yet…what if it was true? What if the wind
outside had brought something magic along with
it, something other than snow and power failures?

A handsome stranger.

And her own past.

Dear Reader,

Baby birds are chirping, bees are buzzing and the tulips are beginning to bud. Spring is here, so why not revive the winter-weary romantic in you by reading four brand-new love stories from Silhouette Romance this month.

What's an old soldier to do when a bunch of needy rug rats and a hapless beauty crash his retreat? Fall in love, of course! Follow the antics of this funny little troop in *Major Daddy* (#1710) by Cara Colter.

In *Dylan's Last Dare* (#1711), the latest title in Patricia Thayer's dynamite THE TEXAS BROTHERHOOD miniseries, a cranky cowboy locks horns with his feisty physical therapist and then learns she has a little secret she soon won't be able to hide!

Jordan Bishop wants to dwell in a castle and live happily ever after, but somehow things aren't going as she's planned, in *An Heiress on His Doorstep* (#1712) by Teresa Southwick. This is the final title in Southwick's delightful IF WISHES WERE…miniseries in which three friends have their dreams come true in unexpected ways.

When a bookworm meets her prince and discovers she's a real-life princess, will she be able to make her own happy ending? Find out in *The Secret Princess* (#1713) by Elizabeth Harbison.

Celebrate the new season, feel the love and join in the fun by experiencing each of these lively new love stories from Silhouette Romance!

Mavis C. Allen
Associate Senior Editor

Please address questions and book requests to:
Silhouette Reader Service
U.S.: 3010 Walden Ave., P.O. Box 1325, Buffalo, NY 14269
Canadian: P.O. Box 609, Fort Erie, Ont. L2A 5X3

The
Secret Princess

ELIZABETH HARBISON

SILHOUETTE *Romance* ®
Published by Silhouette Books
America's Publisher of Contemporary Romance

To Johnny Tillotson: Romantic idol to millions and
my own Hilton hallway buddy. Here's to you, Johnny.

 SILHOUETTE BOOKS

ISBN 0-373-19713-6

THE SECRET PRINCESS

This edition published by arrangement with Harlequin Books S.A.

® and TM are trademarks of Harlequin Books S.A., used under license.
Trademarks indicated with ® are registered in the United States Patent
and Trademark Office, the Canadian Trade Marks Office and in other
countries.

Visit Silhouette at www.eHarlequin.com

Printed in U.S.A.

Books by Elizabeth Harbison

Silhouette Romance

A Groom for Maggie #1239
Wife Without a Past #1258
Two Brothers and a Bride #1286
True Love Ranch #1323
*Emma and the Earl #1410
*Plain Jane Marries the Boss #1416
*Annie and the Prince #1423
*His Secret Heir #1528
A Pregnant Proposal #1553
Princess Takes a Holiday #1643
The Secret Princess #1713

Silhouette Special Edition

Drive Me Wild #1476
Midnight Cravings #1539

*Cinderella Brides

Silhouette Books

Lone Star Country Club
Mission Creek Mother-To-Be

ELIZABETH HARBISON

has been an avid reader for as long as she can remember. After devouring the Nancy Drew and Trixie Belden series in grade school, she moved on to the suspense of Mary Stewart, Dorothy Eden and Daphne du Maurier, just to name a few. From there it was a natural progression to writing, although early efforts have been securely hidden away in the back of a closet.

After authoring three cookbooks, Elizabeth turned her hand to writing romances and hasn't looked back. Her second book for Silhouette Romance, *Wife Without a Past,* was a 1998 finalist for the Romance Writers of America's prestigious RITA® Award in the Best Traditional Romance category.

Elizabeth lives in Maryland with her husband, John, daughter Mary Paige, and son Jack, as well as two dogs, Bailey and Zuzu. She loves to hear from readers and you can write to her c/o Box 1636, Germantown, MD 20875.

LONG-LOST PRINCESS FOUND...
IN DENTYTOWN!

Maryland—Residents of Dentytown were
shocked yesterday to learn that Amy Scott,
owner of a modest travel bookshop, might,
in fact, be the missing Princess Amelia of
Lufthania. Details are sketchy, but one witness
reported that "a totally hot guy," who said he
worked for Crown Prince Wilhelm of Lufthania,
showed up at Ms. Scott's bookshop personally
to give her the news and escort her to her native
country. The witness also reported that Ms. Scott
was "cautious" about his claims and agreed to
have a DNA test. There is no official word yet,
but royal watchers are keeping an eager eye
on the news from the tiny Alpine
country to learn if they've had
a real princess in their
midst for 25 years.

Prologue

Twenty-Five Years Ago

"We have to go now, tonight. As the legitimate heirs to the throne, you and Amelia are in terrible danger."

Princess Lily of Lufthania looked at her husband and hoped her eyes didn't show the fear she felt. "I know. I don't want to leave my country but…" Tears burned her eyes. "We have no choice. Father has friends in Washington, D.C. We'll be safe there until we find a new home." As if any place but Lufthania would ever feel like home.

Georg put his hand over hers. "You will be happy again. I swear it."

She gave a small smile. "As long as I'm with you."

He nodded but looked unconvinced. "We'll have a brand-new start. We can make up new names for ourselves, new histories. How many people get a chance like that?"

They both knew the answer: *only those unlucky enough to have their home stormed by hostile forces who would as soon kill them as look at them.*

"I suppose we're lucky," she said, trying to believe it. Commander Maxim's soldiers had already killed her widowed father, and although Maxim had said he would spare Princess Lily and give her a country home that had been in the family for many years, she knew it would be little more than a house arrest at best, and a setup for murder at worst. No, Lily and her husband and daughter needed to escape before the commander's coup was complete and the airlines were under his control. "I'm certain the people will not stand for this new regime. Before we know it, we will be free to return."

His gaze was serious. "You do know we might never return."

"Yes." Her father had been very pointed in telling her that, right before he pressed a large diamond ring into her hand and made her promise to leave the country, to flee to safety and sell the ring in order to start a new life.

"But Papa," she had said, *"you can come with us."*

"No, my sweet." He drew her to him in a strong embrace. *"I cannot leave my country. I have lived for my duties to the people and I will die for them, if need*

be.'' He saw her objection before she voiced it, and put a finger to her lips. *"No, it is not the same for you. You must be safe. You must keep my granddaughter safe. One day you will return to the throne. In the meantime, you must be sure they cannot find you. They may view the rightful heir to the throne as a threat."* It was as if he'd known he was going to die. Perhaps he had.

Lily returned her attention to her husband. "I'm certain we will return. Right always wins in the end."

He looked into her eyes and smiled. "So idealistic. Is it any wonder that I love you so much?"

Her eyes burned but she was out of tears. "I love you too, Georg. More than I can say."

Their daughter, little Princess Amelia, stirred in her cot. In two and a half months, Amelia would turn three. By then, her entire world would be different. She would no longer sleep in the butter-yellow nursery with the soft cotton sheets that had been her mother's and her grandmother's before that; she would no longer run into her grandpa's arms every morning before breakfast; she would no longer have a future planned and destined for her, with assurances of home, food, safety and security.

And she would no longer be a princess.

Chapter One

Amy Scott turned the sign on the door around so Sorry, We're Closed faced the icy winter landscape outside. Not that many people in Dentytown cared if they were closed this time of year. In the winter months, Blue Yonder Travel Books did most of its business over the Internet rather than from customers in the tiny Maryland town.

"Think it's going to keep snowing?" Amy's employee, Mara Hyatt, walked over to the window next to Amy.

"I hope so." Amy sighed and watched the small snowflakes trailing down from the sky. The snow always gave her a sense of peace.

The wind lifted and blew against the glass window hard enough to make Amy step back in surprise. This was no ordinary snow. Something strange was brewing out there. She could feel it. Almost as if the wind was bringing change of some sort.

"Did you package that order for the safari books?" Amy asked, trying to distract herself from the feeling of premonition.

"Right there." Mara pointed to a pile of neatly packed and labeled boxes. "You want me to wait for the shipping company?"

Amy waved the notion away. "No, I've got some things to do, anyway. Go on. Enjoy the snow. Go sledding."

"Okay." Mara gathered her coat and scarf. "Call me if you need me."

Amy smiled. "Will do."

The bell on the door trilled as Mara left, and Amy stood there for several moments, shivering. She couldn't say if it was the cold or the strange apprehension about the storm that did it, but she was glad she had some work to help take her mind off of it. She was nearly finished balancing the books when a strong wind lifted and the lights flickered off.

Amy froze. The only sound was the gentle ting of the bells over the door, swaying in the whispers of wind that pushed through the cracks.

She let out a long breath. It was just a power failure. Dentytown still had the exposed old-fashioned electrical wires that could be downed by a falling tree branch. That was probably exactly what had happened. Feeling somewhat reassured, she opened the drawer in front of her and felt for a matchbook she knew was there. It was from a restaurant she'd visited in New

York years ago. She'd just seen it in the drawer this afternoon.

She found the matches, struck one and lit the two aromatherapy candles she had on her desk. The room sprang back to life in the unsteady orange glow. She stood up and tried to stretch the tension out of her limbs.

No sooner did she take a single relieved breath than the bells over the door rang again, this time louder as the door was being opened.

Amy turned as a stranger came in.

He must have been over six feet tall, with midnight-black hair that gleamed eerily by the candlelight. His eyes looked dark, though she couldn't be sure, and a hint of shadow on his jaw gave him a shadowed look, like a character in a book who could be either good or evil.

Amy swallowed. "I'm sorry, the store is closed." She felt behind her for the letter opener on the desk.

"I'm not here to shop," he said, his voice deep and deliberate. He had just a hint of some sort of accent. "I'm looking for someone—"

She thought fast. "Oh, you must be Allen's hunting buddy. He's in the back getting his guns together for your trip." She moved around the desk, hoping the stranger didn't notice her shaking hands and jelly legs. "I'll just go get him." She could go out the back door, she decided. The police station was only two blocks away. Someone would be on duty, and she could bring whoever it was back with her.

She was almost to the door when the man said, "I'm looking for Amy Scott."

She stopped and turned around. "Why?"

"Are *you* Amy Scott?"

She glanced at the door, then back at the man, who had not moved since he'd come in. He wasn't advancing on her. If she needed to, she could almost certainly outrun him, if only because she had several yards' head start. "Who wants to know?"

He stepped closer. "But you are, of course. Your face…it's unmistakable."

She automatically lifted a hand to her cheek. "Have we met?"

"No, I don't believe we have." His mouth curved toward a smile but didn't quite make it. In the flickering candlelight he looked the way she'd always imagined Sir Lancelot—a deeply handsome face, sensuous mouth, intelligent eyes, but a stature that implied such power that he was almost intimidating. Almost.

He moved toward her and gently lowered her hand from her face. "My God, you're even more beautiful than I'd imagined."

Her heart hammered in response to his touch, even as her brain told her to back off and be prepared to call the authorities in case this was some crazy guy off the street.

"You tried to imagine what I'd look like?" she heard herself ask.

"All my life."

Though the door was closed, when the wind lifted

again outside, Amy imagined she felt it finger through her hair and tingle down her back. "Why?" she asked, standing her ground by the back door. "Who are you?"

"Forgive me," he said, smiling the kind of thousand-megawatt smile usually reserved for movie stars. "I'm not explaining myself very well. I am," did he hesitate? "Franz Burgess. I am in the royal service of the Crown Prince of Lufthania."

"Lufthania?" Last year she had spent a frustrating month trying to locate a travel book on Lufthania for the Bradleys, a local couple who were always looking for unusual and obscure travel destinations. She had been unsuccessful in finding a book, but she'd learned just enough about the small Alpine country to pique her curiosity.

"You have heard of Lufthania?" he asked, not necessarily surprised, but he watched her with keen interest.

"Just barely. Who did you say you were?"

"I am secretary to the Crown Prince. Looking for, well, you might say a long-lost relative."

Amy raised an eyebrow. "Then you must have taken a wrong turn somewhere. There's no royalty here."

"Don't be so sure."

"Oh, I'm sure." The lights flickered on and Amy said a silent thanks to the Chesapeake Electric Company. "Oh. That's better." She blew out her candles and felt more confident now that the power was on.

That is, until she looked at Franz Burgess and saw what the candlelight had barely revealed.

Her first crazy thought was that he was one of the most handsome men she had ever seen. It was that simple. His eyes, which had held so much expression even in the dark, were so vibrant a green that it seemed as if light came from inside of them. His hair was wavy and haphazard, a rich chocolate brown touched with auburn lights from the same sun that had tanned his skin.

He was a little bit younger than she'd initially thought, perhaps in his mid-thirties. Faint lines bracketed his mouth and fanned out from the corners of his eyes, but rather than aging him, they gave his face just the ruggedness it needed to keep from being too pretty.

"As I was saying," he said, "I'm here in the prince's service, looking for a lost relative."

"A lost relative," she repeated flatly. "Of royalty." She stared at him for a moment before asking, "Are you an actor?" That would explain the slick good looks, the smooth delivery of an absurd story. Someone had hired him as a practical joke.

He looked puzzled. "I beg your pardon?"

"Did one of my friends send you here with this crazy story?" That had to be it. Someone remembered her search for books on Lufthania and thought it would be funny to resurrect the place.

"I'm sorry, I don't understand."

"Neither do I," she said. "My birthday isn't for two months."

"On the contrary," he said, his gaze even. "Your birthday was the day before yesterday."

The silence that followed was brief but shuddering.

"What are you talking about?" Her nerves went tight. "My birthday is in almost two months. January twenty-ninth."

He gave a short nod, as if he knew better but wouldn't bother with such small details right now. "Let me explain why I'm here. Why I've been looking for you."

"You have."

He nodded. "For a very long time, actually."

A tremor rumbled through her. "Okay, what do you want? Special orders can take several weeks, you know."

"I'm not here to order anything. My business with you is personal."

Gooseflesh rose on her arms and she ran her hands over them. "What personal business could you possibly have with me, Mr. Burgess?"

His gaze was steady. "What I've come to tell you might seem unbelievable to you, but it's true, and I believe you'll consider it very good news."

Amy's muscles tensed. "So what is it?"

He glanced at her desk. "Perhaps you should sit down."

"That doesn't sound like good news."

He smiled. "Sometimes good news can make you weak in the knees as well."

She bet this guy knew a lot about making women

weak in the knees. "I'll be fine," she said, defying her own reaction to him more than his suggestion that she might go weak. "Spill it."

He raised an eyebrow. "I'm sorry?"

Now it was her turn to smile. "Spill it. Your news. I'm ready."

"All right." He took a breath, then cocked his head slightly and looked at her for a moment before saying, "I'm here on behalf of your country."

She hesitated. "Funny, you don't look like Uncle Sam."

"Not America. Lufthania." He paused for a moment to let that sink in. He watched her closely as he added in a careful tone, "The country where you were born. The country of your blood family."

Her face turned cold, then her shoulders, her arms and, in a rush, the rest of her. For a moment, she couldn't speak. No one ever talked about her biological relatives. She knew nothing about them except that her parents had died in a car accident that she'd survived. Just under three years old, she was taken to Kendell County Hospital, where her adoptive mother, Pamela Scott, had worked as a nurse on the night shift.

The authorities had tried to identify her parents to no avail. No missing-persons reports ever surfaced, no alerts for missing children. It was as if they didn't exist at all. The only reason they knew Amy's name, or thought they did, was because one of the paramedics on the scene had heard the woman saying the name repeatedly before she died. They concluded that Amy must have been the child's name.

Pamela Scott had taken to Amy immediately, working extra shifts to nurse her back to health. When no family could be traced, she and her husband, Lyle, a very successful attorney, had become Amy's foster parents. After several years they were finally able to make the adoption final.

Amy found her voice. "If this is a joke, it isn't funny."

He moved closer to her and put his hands on her shoulders, looking into her eyes. "I assure you, it isn't a joke. Now, why don't you sit down and let me tell you what brought me to you?" He guided her to her chair and she sat like an obedient child. "I only ask that you hear me out with an open mind."

She glanced behind him. "Perhaps it would be wise of me to listen with an open door as well."

He smiled. "You're quite safe, I assure you."

She gestured toward him. "Okay, I'm listening."

He took a breath. "You are the heir to the throne of Lufthania."

A moment passed. "Doesn't Lufthania already have someone on the throne?"

He gave a short nod. "A crown prince who wants to return the throne to the rightful heir after his parents stole it nearly three decades ago."

"Sort of like returning a lost wallet, huh?"

"This is no joke."

She could see he meant it. "Okay. So where are the parents who stole the throne? Aren't they going to be miffed that he's giving it back?"

His face remained impassive. "They're both dead.

The princess died ten years ago of cancer. Her husband, who was much older than she, passed away two years ago of natural causes.''

"Oh." Amy felt she shouldn't have been flip. "Sorry, I—well, why don't you tell me how this led you to me?"

"As I've indicated, twenty-five years ago, there was a political revolution, a coup d'état, in Lufthania. A very distant cousin thought the throne was legitimately his, since it had been taken away from his family several hundred years back owing to the fact that the only heir was not blood, but a foundling.''

"Adopted?"

He nodded. "Exactly. Although that is not a term they used in the sixteenth century."

Amy frowned. "So this descendant of an adopted heir decided to take back what he thought would have been his right, had his ancestor been accepted three hundred years earlier?"

"Yes."

"It sounds like Shakespeare."

He smiled. "Shakespeare could have given it a much tidier ending."

"What was the ending?"

"Prince Josef was removed from the throne and killed by overenthusiastic soldiers for the opposition."

"What about his wife?"

He shook his head. "She had died years before in a riding accident. But his daughter, Princess Lily, escaped the country with her husband and their young daughter. Very few people knew where they'd gone, and not one person knew all of their movements, because it could have compromised their safety. But I have traced their path to the United States.''

She was skeptical. ''How? It seems to me they wouldn't have wanted to be traceable.''

''They didn't. But it's been so long now and the political climate of Lufthania has changed so much— it is now a democracy—that people are finally willing to talk about what they know.''

''People who knew them are still alive?''

He nodded, and she noticed a haunted look in his eye. ''Lily and her family stayed with friends in Washington, D.C., for a while, before shedding their identities entirely and leaving the city. Sort of like your witness protection program, you understand?''

Amy nodded.

''They stayed in the city for some months before picking their destination and leaving. Their friends never expected to hear from them again, so when they didn't, they were not alarmed.''

''They never heard about an accident involving people who couldn't be identified but who fit the descriptions?'' She very nearly said *our descriptions* but caught herself.

''No. When the accident occurred, it didn't make national headlines because it was assumed all identifying papers had merely been lost in the explosion of the car. The authorities checked national databases for missing people for more than a year afterward, but nothing ever came of it.'' His voice softened. ''But, then, you already know that part of the story.''

Amy swallowed a very large lump in her throat, but it didn't go away. She felt her lower lip tremble, and pressed her lips together to stop it. She didn't want to cry. She'd spent a long time *not* crying about those missing first years and the parents she'd lost. Somehow it had felt disloyal to Pamela and Lyle Scott to even think about her biological parents, and the fact that Pamela and Lyle never mentioned them either seemed to corroborate that.

So for more than two decades Amy had dismissed those thoughts from her mind over and over again until, finally, she rarely had them anymore.

And now this man—this *stranger*—came in and churned all those emotions up again.

Seeing her distress, Franz pulled a handkerchief from his pocket and handed it to her. "I'm so sorry to touch on such a tender subject, but you need to know that you belong in Lufthania."

Amy dabbed her eyes with his handkerchief and tried to smile. "Look, you must have the wrong person. I'm no princess."

"As I understand it, you have no memory whatsoever of your life before the accident."

"Who told you that?"

"I've done a lot of research in trying to find you."

"I'm not sure I like that."

He gave a half shrug. "It was necessary. Now, you can't very well say that you're not the princess if you don't remember who you are."

"It just defies logic," she argued. "I have an ordinary life. An ordinary business, with ordinary bills that need to be paid.''

He smiled. ''That doesn't preclude your heritage.''

She sighed. ''Look, what would royalty have been doing driving through Dentytown in an old Chevy, for Pete's sake?''

''They didn't want to be found.''

''Well, surely they could have traced my mother's DNA during—'' she paused and took a short breath ''—during the autopsy.''

He shook his head. ''Not in those days. It would, of course, be possible now. In fact, that's exactly what I have in mind.''

She stepped back involuntarily, as if he might pull a syringe out of his pocket. ''What exactly do you have in mind?''

''For you to go back to Lufthania with me and have your blood tested with DNA samples from your grandparents. The laboratory can have the results back four to seven days after the test.''

She gave a shout of laughter, then, when he remained solemn, asked, ''Are you serious?''

''Quite.''

''You want me to go to Lufthania? Just leave my life behind and go jetting off with some guy I don't even know on the basis of a ten-minute story I find unbelievable? No thanks.'' She laughed and tried to imagine her parents' reaction to such an announcement and laughed again. They'd probably be up from Florida within three hours. ''No way.''

''Are you not even a little curious?''

"No. This is crazy. And even if I were, why couldn't I just give blood here? Go to my own doctor and have him take blood and send it to your lab technicians or whatever? Why on earth should I have to leave the country for such a routine test?"

"Because we are not talking about a simple paternity test," he explained patiently. "This is to confirm your position as royalty. The reigning monarch of a nation. There must be witnesses to the blood test, witnesses who can confirm and swear that you were present as the test subject."

She still didn't get it. "Can't you have witnesses here?"

"It would be impractical to fly a number of witnesses here rather than to simply fly you there. To be honest with you, I didn't anticipate having to persuade you to go."

"What woman in her right mind would just blindly go along with this?"

"One who is open to the facts. One who wants to know where she comes from."

"Well, I *do* want to know, of course. But I'm not prepared to just jet off to a foreign country and dive in as the long-lost princess when I don't even speak the language. I don't even know what the language in Lufthania is!"

"It's German."

"Well, there you go. I don't speak or understand one word of German. How could I possibly become the princess there?"

"Your birthright has nothing to do with the language you speak. You have been in this country for nearly a quarter of a century. Naturally, much of your heritage has been lost to you.''

''Much of my heritage,'' she repeated, unconvinced. She thought of her father, always practical. What would he do? One answer hit her suddenly. ''I'm not even sure of *your* heritage. Do you have any proof that you are who you say you are?'' She should have asked that the moment he walked through the door.

''Of course.'' He stopped and pulled a wallet out of the inner pocket of his dark overcoat. He handed it to her.

On top, there was a photo identification card with his name and vital statistics, as well as the designation Secretary in Service of His Highness, Prince Wilhelm of Lufthania.

Amy wouldn't have known a legitimate Arizona driver's license if she saw it, much less a legitimate Secretary in the Service of His Highness, Prince Wilhelm of Lufthania ID card, but she couldn't suppress a laugh. ''Did you get this at some carnival or something?''

He did not smile. ''I did not.''

She handed it back to him. ''Well, sorry, but that doesn't convince me of anything. I'm not leaving the country on the basis of your story so far.''

''And if I gave you satisfactory evidence of my contention?''

He looked so serious that she had to stop and think. ''Maybe—*maybe*—I would agree to this crazy plan. But I would need to have pretty hard evidence.''

He looked amused. "You're very like your mother, Amelia."

"It's Amy," she corrected him absently.

"No, it's Amelia. Princess Amelia Louisa Gretchen May." He smiled sadly. "However, your parents simply called you Amé."

"Amé," she repeated, numb. The name, as he pronounced it, held some resonance for her. It echoed through cobwebbed chambers of her memory. Amé. Amy. She could almost hear it. It was easy to see why the paramedics had assumed the woman was saying "Amy."

For her own part, Amy had not spoken a word for the first four months after the accident. After ruling out autism, psychologists had attributed her silence to the trauma. If Mr. Burgess's story was correct, though, it could conceivably be because she hadn't understood the language.

But that was impossible.

Wasn't it?

"Are you all right?" he asked, concern etched in his features. "Can I get you some water? Do you have brandy here?"

Despite her shock, she had to smile at the idea of having a bottle stashed somewhere. "No, I don't. I'm okay. It's just…obviously, this is all a bit of a shock. Not that I believe it," she was quick to add. "But I'm willing to listen if you'll tell me everything."

He nodded. "I will. But not now. You look very tired tonight."

Now that he mentioned it, she was exhausted. This

brief conversation had taken a toll on her energy. Besides, she needed time to call her parents, to get their advice and opinions. It was late now, but she'd call, anyway. "Can you come back tomorrow morning? With this proof you say you have?"

"Of course. For now, why don't you let me take you home? I have a car right out front." He gestured toward the wide plate-glass window, through which Amy could see a long black limousine parked out front.

"No, thanks. I only live a couple of blocks away and, frankly, I could use the walk."

"It's quite inclement," he pointed out.

The snow was falling heavily now, billowed by the occasional gust of wind.

"Then you'd better get that boat out of here before it gets stuck," Amy said. "Come back tomorrow. I'll be here from 10:00 a.m. until at least five or six."

"I'll be here early. I hope you'll be ready to go." Before she could object, he raised a hand. "Just in case the evidence is sufficiently persuasive to you. You must be open to that possibility."

He was a hard man to refuse. "Okay. I'll try. But I'm not making any guarantees."

"Very well." He gave a short bow. "Until tomorrow." With one last lingering gaze, he turned and left the shop. The driver hopped out of the car to open the door for him, but he waved him off and opened it himself. He looked back at the shop before closing the door behind him, and for one insane moment, Amy wondered if she'd dreamed the whole thing.

Then the wind blew again, pushing the door open. Amy ran to close it. The small spots of cold snow that landed on her skin assured her that she was awake.

She closed the door and turned the dead bolt. How was it she'd managed to forget to do that earlier? She always locked the bolt after she turned the sign to Closed.

She leaned her back against the door and closed her eyes. The only thing wrong with his story—the only part that didn't tug at her heart—was the part about being royal. If he had come along telling her he had evidence of her biological family and that they lived in Cleveland, she would have been thrilled. But this business of royalty tipped the story into the realm of fairy tale, making it something she couldn't entirely believe.

Yet…what if it were true? What if the wind outside had brought something magic along with it, something other than snow and power failures?

A handsome stranger.

And her own past.

Chapter Two

Franz Burgess, known as Will to his friends, went outside into the damp, cold air and got into the waiting limousine. He'd hoped to feel relieved by this point, but he'd known, going into this, that he might be disappointed. With everything he knew about Amy Scott—and he knew a great deal—he should have known her intelligence would make her cynical, at least give her a cynical reaction to his story.

One thing he had not known, or prepared himself for, was his own reaction to *her*. From the moment he'd laid eyes on her he'd been captivated by her. He could have stayed all night, watching her eyes flash when she spoke, listening to her voice, observing her movements and the way her clothes hugged the soft contours of her body.

It wasn't simply that she was attractive. He had

plenty of access to beautiful women. At times, he was even *tired* of beautiful women. They all seemed so vacant. But Amy Scott was different. Her coloring was like that of many women from his country, the pale skin and faintly pink cheeks. Yet she had something different, something extra. It was an unexplainable quality of magnetism that he'd rarely encountered. It was easy to imagine himself watching her for many years to come.

If only he could persuade her that the story he'd told her was true. She was so perfect for the role. Her sharp intelligence, combined with her beauty, would make her an excellent princess. Yet she was skeptical. And despite financial difficulties that he knew about, she was strong enough to resist the temptation of being told she was a princess and would thus have no more bills and debtors to worry about.

So he was going to have to bring out documentation, to try to convince her to accompany him back to Lufthania. It wasn't going to be easy, he knew that already. But he'd budgeted time for that possibility.

However, he hadn't budgeted time, or prepared himself mentally, for the possibility that he *couldn't* convince her. That would be a disaster for him. Yet it was looking entirely possible that he wouldn't be able to. He didn't know what he'd do if she didn't come back to Lufthania with him.

His entire life depended on it.

The first thing Amy did after Franz Burgess left was call her parents. They both got on the line and for half an hour they discussed the situation. Amy was surprised that her parents didn't immediately dismiss the idea that she might be a princess.

To the contrary, her mother was ready to believe it. "I've always thought you were more regal than most people," she said.

"What are you talking about?"

"Well, you were never too fond of doing the dishes, and it was darn near impossible to get you to clean your room." She laughed. "I always thought it was a queen complex, but princess will do."

Amy was glad for the levity. In the end, they agreed that Amy would see Franz Burgess's evidence in the morning and make a judgment based on that. If he was on the up-and-up, they reasoned, he must have some pretty compelling evidence. She could hear him out and call them back with the additional facts.

Meanwhile, her father would call the Lufthania embassy and see if he could verify the existence of Franz Burgess.

After that, they would decide together what Amy should do.

This plan made Amy feel a lot better, and she spent the rest of the night looking for any information she could find on Lufthania.

First, she checked her stock for any books that might make even slight mention of Lufthania. Since it was a very small country and didn't hold the international cachet of, say, Monaco, no books were devoted to it entirely, but she recalled several references to it in some of the books on Germany and Switzerland. It was little more than a footnote, but when she looked through an out-of-print volume on the region, she was able to find a slender chapter devoted to the country and its history.

The book was written in the late 1940s and had no reference to the coup d'état Franz Burgess had told her about. However, it did go into a bit of detail on the royal family, Prince Josef, Princess Lily and their daughter, Princess Amelia. The young princess was pictured playing in the snow with a St. Bernard puppy.

It was difficult to distinguish the girl's facial features, so when Amy imagined she looked familiar—perhaps similar to the image mirrors had held of Amy some twenty years ago—she chalked it up to an overactive imagination.

Still, she read and reread the pages, scouring for every mention of Lufthania, and she kept returning to the picture of the little girl.

Then she tried the Internet. The story of the coup was there, but no pictures. She also found some official government documents that appeared to be written in a Germanic language, and a couple of personal travel diaries written by people who had happened through a corner of Lufthania on their way to someplace more famous, but that was all. There was nothing solid to persuade Amy to believe Franz Burgess's story.

Yet as difficult as it was to believe it could be true, it managed to touch Amy's heartstrings. What could be better for the girl who had spent a lifetime wondering who she really was and where—if anywhere—

she'd truly fit in, than to find her family history and home all in one shot? To find a long, documented family tree? One with golden apples, no less.

She read through the night and far into the wee hours of the morning, stopping occasionally to refill her coffee mug, or gaze at the snow in the hazy glow of the street lamp. She'd always enjoyed the cold weather more than the heat. Did that mean anything? Was it significant somehow? Did it prove the fantastic story?

The questions swirled around in her mind like snow on the wind until her eyelids grew heavy and the words began to blur before her.

She fell asleep without even realizing it until the sunny white glare of morning cut through the store windows and woke her just in time to see the long black limo pull up outside.

He was back.

Amy stood up quickly, raked her hand through her hair and threw open her desk drawer to look for a piece of gum to make up for not having time to brush her teeth.

He tapped on the door just as she was tossing the wrapper into the trash.

She took a deep breath and tried to compose herself before walking, as regally as she could, to the door and letting him in.

"Good morning," he said, a smile in his eyes. "I hope I didn't wake you."

She feigned surprise. "Wake me? Of course not. I've been here for at least an hour."

"At least." He did smile then, and reached out and touched her very briefly on the cheek. "You appear to have the imprint of your computer keyboard on your face."

"What?" She lifted her hand to her cheek.

"And you haven't changed your clothes since last night. Did you fall asleep here reading about Lufthania?"

An objection lodged in her throat, but she swallowed it. Why bother pretending she wasn't curious? "Weren't you expecting me to check up on your story?"

"As a matter of fact, I was." He held up a valise. "Which is why I brought you all of the documentation I had that led me to you." He dropped the valise on the desk and pulled off his expensive-looking leather driving gloves, one by one, stuffing them into the pockets of his camel-colored overcoat.

"That's for me to look through?"

"Please." He made an expansive gesture. "Be my guest."

"Why didn't you bring all of this with you in the first place?"

He gave a brief smile. "I first had to be convinced you were the one. *Then* I could set about convincing you, although, to tell you the truth, I didn't think you would need much persuasion." For just a moment, he looked grim. "I hope what I have here will convince you."

"We'll see." She gave a dry laugh. "I don't know

what kind of women you know, but I don't know anyone who wouldn't approach this with caution.''

She took the valise and sat down with it on the other side of the desk. As she unzipped it, she had half a thought that it might not be safe to open anything brought by a man she didn't know and who—if his story was false, as it must be—might well be nuts.

But it was already open before she could stop herself, and her curiosity was rewarded with a large, neat stack of papers and photographs.

He walked around behind her and bent over her. "If I may explain," he said. "This is the route Princess Lily and her husband, Georg, along with you, took out of Lufthania. As you can see, they were not yet hiding their identities, so this is unrefuted documentation.''

Amy looked at what could have been a travel itinerary for any of her bookstore customers who were planning a vacation. It was hard to believe it was the escape route of a princess and her family.

"Next you have the affidavit of Ambassador Whisle, and his wife, who took Princess Lily, Georg and Amé into their Washington, D.C., home.''

Determined to be thorough, Amy took the pages in hand and read carefully as he explained each and every piece of paper. Every once in a while, she found herself distracted by his proximity, and the clean, spicy scent of his after-shave—a unique and alluring scent, unlike anything she'd ever smelled before. But each time her mind wandered, she forced it back to the papers before her. After all, this could be—

She couldn't even finish the thought. Of course it

couldn't be. It couldn't be anything to do with her. Still, it made for an interesting and romantic story. Perhaps she could put it on her Web site along with recommendations for the books she'd found on Lufthania.

"Amelia?"

"Yes?" she answered absently, then immediately realized her mistake. "Are you talking to me?"

He chuckled softly and nodded. "There is only one Amelia here."

She glanced at him sideways. "Maybe not even that many."

He raised his eyebrows and gave a short nod, the traditional expression of *touché*. "I was going to ask you if you wanted some breakfast. I can send my driver to the shop, if you like."

"No, I'm good. Thanks." She thought of the coffee and gum, which were all she'd had for twelve hours. "Unless you're sending him, anyway?"

He flashed a brilliant smile and held up his index finger. "I'll be back in a moment." She watched him go out the front door, apparently heedless of the cold, and bend down to the passenger window of the limo. It opened and he said something to the driver inside, then stood back up, gave two flat-handed pats on the roof of the car and came back in while the limo edged out of sight. He came back over to her, the crisp scent of cold and snow clinging to him.

"If you've finished reading the affidavit, you can see here the receipt for a car purchased on the afternoon that they left the ambassador's mansion. That car fits the description of the one that was in the accident.''

Amy listened to his story, following along with his visual aids, eyewitness accounts, maps and various other pieces of evidence that made his story seem plausible. She believed he might have accurately traced the movements of the princess and her family to a point, and then moved onto her own history.

''Like your mother, you excelled in literature in college. This course on comparative literature looks quite challenging.''

''Wait a minute—''

He turned a page and raised an eyebrow at her. ''But I see you did have some trouble with mathematics.''

''I did not!'' She was immediately defensive. ''First of all, Professor Tanner lost an assignment that accounted for thirty-three percent of my grade, then penalized me for it, and second of all, that is none of your business.''

''Professor Tanner claims that you never turned the work in.''

Outrage rose in Amy. ''You *talked* to him? You actually contacted my former teachers before you ever even met—'' She stopped when she saw the amusement in his eyes. ''You're kidding, right?'' she asked soberly.

''Right.'' He smiled. ''My apologies.'' He didn't look sorry at all. He flipped through some more pages. ''I see you were also engaged after college to a...Ben Singer.''

"Do you also see that he dumped me for another woman, claiming I was 'emotionally inaccessible'?" she asked sharply.

He leveled a blue gaze on her. "No. Are you?"

"No." She didn't mention that she hadn't had a relationship last longer than a month since, or that her friends joked that they wouldn't take one of her boyfriends seriously unless he made it to day thirty-two. "I'm in full possession of my emotions," she contended.

He laughed. "You seem uncomfortable with personal questions."

She was. "Only because I don't think my private life has anything to do with this."

"On the contrary, I believe your private life has everything to do with your heritage. To say nothing of your royal duties."

She shook her head. "I think it's a bit early still to be talking about my royal duties. I am in no way convinced that my parents are who you say they are. I mean, it's *very* difficult to believe they came so far off the royal course as to end up in Dentytown."

"Keep looking" was all he said, indicating the papers she held.

As he must have predicted, her skepticism was in for a shock when she got to the end of the pile. With only a couple of papers left, he pulled out a stiff piece of paper with "Princess Lily, Lufthan Palace" scrawled across the back in spidery script.

"Here," he said gravely, "is the last known picture taken of Princess Lily. Your mother."

Amy took the faded color photo from him slowly. Her first reaction was that her eyes were playing tricks on her.

Her second reaction was to think this was a dream. This *had* to be a dream.

Because there, in her trembling hand, was a glossy photograph of a woman with long wavy auburn hair, pale blue eyes and a small cleft in her chin. A woman who, if she hadn't *known* better, she would have sworn was herself.

"Okay, whoa, you're going *where?* With *whom?*" Mara's face registered all of the incredulity and skepticism that had been churning in Amy's stomach since Franz Burgess had first walked through her door and told his story.

It wasn't as if she'd just magically gotten over her doubts, but when she'd seen that photograph of Princess Lily, it was as if someone had punched her in the gut. She decided to ignore the lure of logic and take a chance, for once in her life, by getting to the bottom of the story.

"What do your parents think about this?"

"We spent the entire night talking about it," Amy said. "And they're with me—this warrants investigation."

"You've all lost your minds."

"Maybe, but we're not complete fools. My father

did call the embassy and confirm that Franz Burgess is the private secretary to Prince Wilhelm.

"That's a relief. I guess."

"Look," Amy said, sticking the last of her instruction Post-its on the wall next to the desk, "I figure this will make a great story, if nothing else. Think of the publicity we could get for Blue Yonder—maybe I could do an editorial piece for *Coastal Life* or some other magazine. 'I Was a Princess for a Day,' that kind of thing." That wasn't the real reason she was going, but she could barely admit to herself how much she wanted to find her roots, much less share that with someone else.

Mara screwed up her eyebrows. "And you're not going to be devastated if this all turns out to be a hoax?"

"Absolutely not," Amy answered vehemently. "Although I get the feeling this isn't a hoax. A mistake, probably, but I don't think anyone is setting this up as a cruel joke to make me look stupid."

"I can't think of anyone who'd want to do that to you," Mara agreed, then pressed her lips together for a moment before asking, "Have you thought about what you'll do if it turns out to be true?"

Amy stopped shuffling papers for a moment. "What, that I'm a princess?" She dropped the papers into a file folder.

Mara nodded excitedly. "Can you *imagine?*"

Amy paused and tried to imagine. Princess Amy of Lufthania. It was ridiculous enough to make her laugh. "No, I can't imagine. I'd like to, but I just can't."

She sat heavily in her chair and rubbed her eyes. "Oh, Mara, do you think this is crazy? Am I insane to even think about going through with this?"

Mara sat on the edge of the desk and patted Amy's shoulder reassuringly. "To tell you the truth, I'm not so sure this is all that far-fetched."

Amy raised an eyebrow.

"No, I'm serious," Mara said. "You don't know what your life was before the accident when you were three. The dates fit. The physical description fits. Maybe it would be crazy *not* to investigate further."

Those were the very thoughts that had made Amy decide to go. "Thanks," she said, putting her hand on Mara's. "I needed to hear that."

"Anytime. Now, don't you worry about a thing while you're gone. I can handle the store and the orders and anything that might come down the pike. You just go and have some fun, okay? If you don't bring back a crown, you can at least bring back an outrageous tale, huh? And maybe a souvenir or two."

Amy gave a laugh. "Yeah, an 'I went to Lufthania to be a princess but all I got was this lousy T-shirt' T-shirt." She opened the desk drawer to retrieve her cell phone. She dropped it into her purse and said, "I hope this works in Lufthania, just in case I need to call and have you come rescue me."

"There are always local police," Mara said seriously.

"Oh, Mara, I was kidding. Please don't start worrying about me."

"I'm not worrying about you. I'm worrying about *me*."

"You?"

"Yeah, if it turns out you're really a princess and you move off to another country, will I still have a job? Can I be a lady-in-waiting?"

"And waiting and waiting." Amy smiled. "You bet."

The bells on the door chimed, and they both looked up as Franz Burgess walked in.

If possible, he looked even more achingly handsome than he had the night before last, when he'd first come into the shop. He wore a dark sweater, about the color of his hair. It made the green of his eyes seem that much brighter.

"Good morning," he said with a slight bow of the head.

If nothing else, he was extremely well mannered.

"I'm almost ready," Amy said, collecting her bags and trying to remember if there were any last-minute things she had to tell Mara about pending orders.

As she looked around, Mara caught her eye and mouthed "He's gorgeous."

A warm flush, which felt suspiciously like pride, washed over Amy. Yes, he was gorgeous, there was no debating that. But what did that have to do with her? Why should that set her heart pounding?

"Okay." She hoisted her carry-on bag over her shoulder, and her purse on top of that. Then she took a large hardshell suitcase—which, according to old television advertisements, even a gorilla couldn't destroy—in each hand and said, "I'm ready."

"Is that your luggage?"

She glanced at the suitcases, then back at him. "Yes. Is there a problem?"

He laughed and took the heavy cases from her effortlessly. "You really needn't bother bringing anything. All of your needs will be tended to there."

"*All* of them?" Mara asked.

Amy shot her a silencing look.

"Of course. You don't need to bring clothing or—" He smiled. "—accessories. The prince is prepared to give you whatever your heart desires."

"That's very nice of him, but I'm not prepared to be beholden to a prince I've never met." She thought about that for a nanosecond before amending, "I'm not prepared to be beholden to *anyone,* whether I know them or not."

"Very well," he said with a light sigh. "It's my job to see to your comfort."

"In that case, stock the plane with angel food cake," Mara chirped. "It's her favorite."

"Goodbye, Mara," Amy said pointedly. "I'll call you when I arrive."

He opened the door for her, then, as soon as she'd passed him, he turned back to Mara and asked, "What is angel food cake?"

"It's like a big, sweet sponge," she answered with a shrug. "I think it's made with a lot of egg whites. I just buy it at the grocery store."

He nodded, as if taking mental notes. ''Angel food cake. It sounds perfect for such a beautiful woman.''

Mara giggled. She was clearly under the man's spell. As soon as he turned his back, Mara kissed her fingertips and gave Amy the thumbs-up.

Amy rolled her eyes, but inside she knew exactly what Mara meant. Franz Burgess had magnetism on about six different levels. Every time she looked at him he seemed to be better-looking. Just when she got used to the cool green of his eyes, she noticed the sensual curve of his mouth. One smile and she was knocked out by how it transformed his face, taking it from serious and darkly handsome to relaxed and open.

Then there was his voice. Smooth and rich, like warm cocoa, with just a hint of an accent that made him seem exotic. Romantic.

As if that wasn't enough, he had that sly, intelligent humor that Amy had always found irresistible. He seemed to be able to read the truth no matter what she said.

Now, that could be dangerous, she thought.

She hoped she'd be able to keep some comfortable distance from him on the plane. Perhaps with a little luck she could find an empty seat next to a chatty businessman.

And with a little willpower, she would take it.

She should have known it would be a private jet and that they would be the only two traveling. He was working for a prince, ostensibly bringing a long-lost princess back to her homeland. It stood to reason that such important business as that would be conducted on a plush Lear jet, with soft music piped over the speaker system and champagne chilling in a silver bucket of ice.

"Are you a fearful flyer?" he asked as Amy sat down and put her seat belt on.

"No, why?"

"You look nervous."

Oh, great. Why did *he* have to be the first really perceptive man she'd met? "It's probably just the coffee I had this morning."

"Ah." He nodded. "Then I assume you won't be wanting any of the cappuccino Annabelle made."

"Annabelle?"

He nodded in the direction of a door to the back. "She's the chef on board."

Amy smiled, hugely relieved. There was someone else on board besides the captain! "Well, let's invite her to join us."

He looked surprised. "Here?"

"Well, sure." She pointed toward two more plush leather seats like the ones they were sitting in. "There's plenty of room."

He shook his head. "I don't believe she'd be comfortable with such an arrangement."

"Why not?"

"Because, for one thing, she is working. It is not part of her job description to sit with the passengers and chat. You wouldn't join your customers on a trip to Nepal because you sold them the guidebook, would you?''

''Oh, come on, it's hardly the same thing!''

He studied her for a moment. ''Do I make you nervous, Amelia?''

Nervous was hardly the word. He made every nerve in her body tingle with giddy awareness. She felt like a junior-high schoolgirl with a crush. ''I wish you wouldn't call me that.''

He gave a nod of concession. ''I apologize. Amy. Perhaps you would like some champagne to combat your agitation.''

The plane began to taxi down the runway. A nervous buzz rushed through Amy's chest. She wasn't *afraid* of flying, but she wasn't completely comfortable with it, either.

She eyed the champagne bottle in the silver bucket. ''No, thank you. I think I'd better keep my wits about me.''

''It's a long flight. Your wits may need a rest after a while.''

She had to laugh. ''You take care of your wits, and I'll take care of mine.''

The plane lifted into the air. Amy looked out the window and watched the land drop away beneath them. Soon they were in the clouds, then, miraculously, above them, soaring into…well, into the blue yonder.

As soon as they were in the air, Amy felt a surge of exhilaration. She'd never left the country before, though she'd gotten her passport five years ago ''just in case.'' Who would have believed that "just in case" would end up meaning "just in case a handsome stranger comes along and tells you you're the princess of a foreign country"?

The door opened and a beautiful, slender blond woman wheeled a cart into the room.

"Good afternoon, sir, ma'am," she said in careful English, giving a slight curtsey. "Here are the pastries you asked for." She locked the wheels of the cart.

"Thank you, Annabelle," he said. "What time is dinner?"

"Will seven o'clock eastern time be too late?"

He looked at Amy with a raised eyebrow. "Does that suit you?"

"Great." She looked at Annabelle. "Thank you so much."

Annabelle smiled, gave a bow to Franz and retreated back through the door.

"She seems nice," Amy said, unable to think of something more clever.

"She's an excellent pastry chef," he said. "You must try one of her chocolate éclairs." He got out of his seat and went to the cart, piling a small china plate with lots of delicious-looking confections.

He brought them back and set them on the table between his chair and Amy's. "It's one of the only things that makes flying tolerable," he said, lifting a chocolate croissant and taking a large bite.

"Are you a nervous flyer?" Amy asked, surprised that someone who worked in a diplomatic capacity that must involve travel could be nervous about flying.

He paused for only a moment. "I could deny it, I suppose, but it would probably become evident all too soon, anyway."

For some reason she found that endearing. "So the champagne is here because—"

"It helps." He nodded, with a self-effacing smile. "Some."

"Thank goodness," Amy said.

He looked at her. "What did you think it was for?"

She felt her face grow warm. "I—I didn't know." She shrugged unconvincingly.

"Did you think I had set the stage for some sort of seduction?" he asked, looking more amused than her ego appreciated.

"You wouldn't be the first man to try something like that."

"Indeed not, I'm sure." He was flat-out smiling now.

"I mean with a woman in general, not just with me," she added, realizing she was protesting too much.

"Amy, would you have me believe that no man has ever tried to seduce you?" he asked in a voice that would have been an ideal start to doing just that.

For a moment, Amy wished she could simply step back two minutes in time so that she had never opened this particular line of conversation. She had no clever response, so instead she said, "You're the one with notes on my entire life, I'm sure there's *nothing* I can tell you that you don't already know."

"Challenge me," he said, still smiling.

"It would only bore you," she said, with what she hoped was a secretive smile.

"Nothing about you bores me."

Her romantic history would. And she didn't want to get into that conversation for fear that she would sound too cynical. She was an optimistic person in all other ways, but when it came to romance, she was one-hundred-percent cynic.

"You're a smooth talker, you know that?"

"I'm only honest."

She laughed. "*Very* smooth. I think I'll do a little reading now." She reached into her bag and took out a copy of *Royalty* magazine, which she'd picked up from the large chain bookstore at the airport before leaving.

He went still. "What's that?"

She frowned and looked at the magazine, then back at him. "It's a magazine. Surely they have these in Lufthania." She looked at it, then at him, expecting him to smile.

He didn't. "I'm sure that won't have anything about Lufthania in it, if that's what you're looking for."

"Actually it is," she said, opening the magazine and settling back for a long read. "Someone at the bookstore recommended it to me as having a lot of information about all of the European royals. I wouldn't have thought of it myself, but it occurs to me that this is probably my best bet for getting current information on the country."

His face was very stern. "Lufthania is never included in those kinds of magazines. Perhaps we should turn down the lights and get some sleep.''

Amy laughed. ''It's two o'clock in the afternoon!''

''How about watching a movie?''

''No, I'm fine.''

He looked around. ''I think there's a chessboard here somewhere....''

She laid the magazine down in her lap. ''Look, I don't know you well, but I can tell you're trying to keep me from looking at this magazine. The question is, why?''

''I'm not.'' He stood up and went to the champagne bottle. He removed the wire cap in one swift motion, then popped the cork. ''Champagne?'' he offered, as if the topic hadn't already come up.

''No, thank you.''

''You can't make a man drink alone.'' He poured two glasses.

She laughed and set the glass he handed her down. ''I can't seem to stop him from doing so, either.''

He took a long draw from the wineglass. ''We have some wonderful vineyards in Lufthania, you know.''

''You're changing the subject.''

He set the glass down without looking at her. ''Of course I'm not.''

''Hmm. Then you won't mind if I just read my magazine now.''

''Not at all.'' He gestured vaguely. ''No. Go right ahead.''

''I plan to.''

''I won't stop you.''

"Good."

"Just let me say this one thing. If there's anything about the Lufthanian royalty in there, it should be taken with, how do you say it, a grain of salt."

"Why?"

He made a dismissive gesture. "You know how those reporters are. Always looking for something sensational to write so they can sell more copies."

"Okay." What did *that* mean? What was he afraid she would see? She looked down and opened the magazine, feeling his eyes on her while she read, although every time she looked up, he appeared to be very involved in reading the *Wall Street Journal.*

She was almost finished with the magazine when she finally came upon the article that he clearly didn't want her to see.

The headline spanned two pages and read Crown Prince Wilhelm Doesn't Want the Throne.

The photo directly beneath it—the photo of Prince Wilhelm—was of Franz Burgess.

Chapter Three

Amy's first impulse was to bat him over the head with the rolled-up magazine. But she stifled that impulse, deciding instead to follow her second impulse, to keep quiet and see how long he was willing to keep up this preposterous charade.

She made a show of closing the magazine, and put it in her bag. Then she stretched and gave a broad, leisurely yawn.

Franz watched her from behind his newspaper. She could feel his gaze like little warm pinpricks all over her body even when she wasn't looking at him.

"So," she said, easing back against the buttery leather of her seat. "Tell me about the prince."

He set the paper down and studied her. "Prince Wilhelm?"

"Who else?"

"What do you want to know?" It was a cautious expression he wore on his face, one that said he was used to being circumspect around people he didn't know very well, in case they had ulterior motives.

She almost felt sorry for him. "Well, I found a small blurb on him on the Internet this morning," she said. "From one of those European gossip magazines, I think." She shrugged. "Anyway, it said that Prince Wilhelm—well, perhaps I shouldn't say. I wouldn't want to offend you or your employer."

He arranged his features into a blank expression.

"As you wish."

"On the other hand, it *is* a concern to me. If he's as awful as they say."

A muscle ticked in his jaw. "Why don't you say what's on your mind?"

"Okay. Is Prince Wilhelm really the vicious tyrant the article said he was?"

He frowned and lifted his champagne glass, the only clue to his discomfort. "I'm not aware that anyone feels that way."

"Oh, yes. According to the article, he has all kinds of harebrained schemes for taxation and population control."

He set his glass down hard. "That is absolutely not true."

"No?" She feigned innocence. "But it was right there in black and white."

"Of course it's not true." There was controlled anger in his low tone. "Those infernal tabloids will say anything to sell copies. The prince wants only the best for his country. That's why he sent for you.''

"Is it?"

Anger glinted in his eye. "How can you doubt it?"

. "Because—well, frankly, because of me. Because you—that is, *he*—came and plucked an American bookstore owner out of a tiny rural town with the hopes that she would move to Lufthania and rule the country." The truth of it made her feel a little sad. "It sounds to me like the prince doesn't want to bother anymore and is willing to pawn the job off on just about anyone."

"No," he said firmly. The glint in his eyes was fierce, and it struck Amy that maybe this wasn't the first time he was having this argument. "The monarch is a figurehead only. There is no power, no ruling, whatsoever. The only danger, if you would call it such, is that the monarch would somehow embarrass the country. And, given our size and the fact that we don't often make international news, there's little chance of that."

A cold feeling washed over her. "So you're looking for someone to fill a role. It doesn't matter who it is. An actress would do."

"No, only a *princess* will do."

"Whether she's qualified or not."

"You have the royal blood." He paused to collect himself, and a vein throbbed in his temple. "You need no further qualification."

She gave a short laugh. "I wonder if the people of Lufthania would agree."

"The people of Lufthania," he said in a low, deliberate voice, "want nothing more than to have you back on the throne. The people of Lufthania *need* the morale boost that would provide. It is selfish of you to even contemplate denying them that."

Her jaw dropped. "Selfish? Of *me?*"

He gave a short nod. "It is not only your birthright, it is your *duty*."

His tone was so hard she felt as if she'd been slapped.

"Duty," she said, "doesn't seem to be something *your prince* takes that seriously."

"He takes his duty *very* seriously."

She scoffed pointedly.

"You know nothing about the matter," he said coldly.

"I know more than you think I do."

"Indeed?"

"Indeed." She was angry now. "For instance, I know your prince is a liar."

"A *liar?*"

"Yes, a liar. He misrepresents himself and his intentions."

"That's a strong accusation."

"Yeah, well, if the shoe fits, wear it." She looked him dead in the eye. *"Prince Wilhelm."*

A shuddering silence passed.

"I'm not—"

She wanted to get her say in before he had a chance to manipulate the facts. "Oh, don't even bother to lie again. I know who you are. And it seems to me that the reason your country needs the—what did you call it?—the *morale boost* of a new monarch is because you, Prince Wilhelm, want to quit.''

"I—"

"Yes, you." She grabbed the magazine, opened it to the right page and thrust it onto his lap. "How long did you think you could keep *that* from me? And why would you bother?"

A long, tense moment passed before he said, "I have not *quit*."

"Yes you have. The minute you have a replacement, you're outta there." Several emotions bubbled in her—residual shock, embarrassment, disappointment and even a little awe. "And you'll take just about anyone as that replacement."

He looked down at the magazine for a moment, then back at Amy. "I'll accept only you."

Something about his tone, and his words, sent a thrill through her, even as she tried to maintain her anger. "I don't understand any of this. Why me?"

"I've told you. Because you're the rightful heir to the throne."

"Even if I am, through the technicality of genetics, that doesn't mean I'm the right person for the job. Blood means almost nothing in reality."

"Blood means everything," he said sternly. It is what separates you from the common shop girl."

"I *am* the common shop girl! Unlike you, I have no problem being honest about who I am."

"That's not a fair assessment. I didn't tell you who I was because I was well aware of how difficult my story would be for you to believe, and I thought telling you who *I* was would make it even more unbelievable.''

''You could have brought *this*.'' She thrust the magazine toward him. ''You could have shown me your picture in there.''

''And had you accuse me of being a lookalike, sent by your friends as some sort of birthday gag?''

He was right, that was *exactly* what she would have thought, but she didn't want to give that to him. ''How can you possibly presume to know what I would think or do?''

He gave a dry smile. ''Perhaps you don't realize how carefully I researched before approaching you. I spent months learning about you, studying the choices you've made in your life, and speculating about what kind of person you might be.'' His green eyes softened with a tenderness that was unexpected to her. ''You'd never heard of me, so this was and is all new to you. But I have thought about you, Amelia, every day for weeks.''

Her breath caught in her throat. He was an undeniably charming man. She'd known that before she'd ever boarded the plane, but she was determined not to let him get to her. She was determined not to compromise her values under the enchanting glow of his gaze.

''You don't know me,'' she objected, with less vehemence than she'd hoped.

''No?''

''No!''

''I know that you are not the kind of person to take

her duties lightly.'' A small smile turned his mouth up. "After all, you were the president *and* treasurer of your tenth-grade high school class.''

She remembered. "No one else would run.''

He chuckled softly. "And you didn't want to let your people down. Your classmates,'' he corrected.

She met his eyes. "No, I wanted to go on the tenth-grade ski trip in the Poconos. No treasurer, no funds. It was selfish.''

"I don't believe you.''

"That hardly seems sufficient reason to give me the crown. Europe is teeming with old royal blood. Surely there were scores of people in line, people who would have been every bit as devoted as you imagined I would be. Or more so.''

The silence that took over the next few seconds was nearly deafening.

"None of whom could have solved the problem.''

"The problem?'' Amy asked. "What problem?''

"The problem of…'' He sighed. "My guilt.''

Amy wasn't expecting that. It took her a moment to formulate a response, and even when she did, it wasn't a great one. "Guilt? You mean for not wanting your position on the throne?''

He shook his head and looked pained. "The coup twenty-five years ago was…not a bloodless one.'' He swallowed, but his eyes remained cool. "There was no one left. No one but you.''

He held her gaze for a moment, but she slowly shook her head. "You have the wrong woman.''

"I don't think so," he said in a tone of absolute certainty.

It was already becoming more difficult to fight this beautiful fantasy, but she knew she had to. If only to protect herself from the inevitable letdown. "Look, I can't prove you wrong at the moment, but I know in my heart I'm not the person you've been looking for." Emotion thickened in her throat. "I'm sorry. I know you went to a lot of trouble to come to me and to arrange this blood test, but it's just going to prove what I've said all along. I'm no princess."

He watched her for what seemed like ages, studying her face, her mouth, her eyes. Then he reached out and cupped his hand on her cheek. "If I didn't believe it before, I do now. You are more regal, more *noble,* than anyone I have ever met."

She resisted the urge to close her eyes and sink into the warmth of his touch. "I'm no different from anyone else."

He smiled that movie-star smile. "Princess Amelia, you are too modest." He didn't move his hand.

And she didn't move a muscle, for fear that he would. "You give me more credit than I deserve."

"I'm not sure that's possible," he said, gently sliding his hand through her hair and pulling her close. "I don't know another woman who would resist the offer I've given you."

Her mouth went dry. Their faces were inches apart. One turbulent bump and she'd lose the tenuous balance she had and would land in his lap. "Have you offered it to many of them?"

He cocked his head and looked amused. "You know that isn't what I meant."

She tried to affect the composure she didn't feel. "I don't know you nearly as well as you seem to know me."

"Do you want to?" he asked.

Her voice took on a breathy Marilyn Monroe quality she didn't intend. "I—I don't know."

"Are you easily persuaded?" he asked, his voice barely more than a whisper itself.

She didn't point out that she wasn't too hard a sell, since she was on the plane with him. Instead she said, "Every year on January 1, I make a resolution to strengthen my willpower."

He lifted an eyebrow but said nothing.

"And every year around January 10 I give up trying."

He laughed. "Then don't try. Willpower is an overrated asset. You have far better ones."

She swallowed. "I do?"

He nodded. "You do." And before she could object, or even think to try, he pulled her into his arms and kissed her.

Her body reacted before her mind had a chance to object.

She had been kissed before, but the moment his lips touched hers, it felt like the first time. As if what she'd experienced before were not kisses, but fumbling adolescent attempts at kisses. Everything that had happened before in her romantic life sank away like a barely remembered dream.

Suddenly *this* was her reality.

Never before had she experienced the physical rush that washed over her, her heart pounding so hard against her rib cage it felt as if it might crack, the explosion of sensation that took over and froze her mind, and the dizzying sense of urgency.

It felt wonderful. He was delicious. And warm. And strong. And the unusual, but distinct scent of his after-shave was intoxicating.

Trying to resist him felt like trying to walk straight after consuming a bottle of vodka, but Amy made the effort.

She drew back and asked, in what felt like a drunken slur, "What are you doing?" Her head was still swimming with the pleasurable sensation, and if he had taken her wordlessly back into his arms, she would have been powerless to resist.

But he didn't. Instead, he appeared maddeningly composed. "Isn't this done in America?"

"Yes." She nodded, buying time to try to come up with a clever response. She couldn't. "By people who know each other."

His mouth cocked into a half smile. "Did I not introduce myself?"

"Actually, no, *Your Highness*—" she paused for emphasis "—you did not. Not with any degree of truth, that is."

He dipped his head. "Then allow me now. I am Wilhelm De Beurghoff, crown prince of Lufthania." He took her hand. "Soon to be the *former* crown prince of Lufthania, that is. You may call me Will."

Her hand was warm in his, and though she thought she should pull it back, she couldn't bring herself to do so. "Will, huh?" Her voice was weak from excitement, but she tried to sound normal. "I like that much better than Franz."

"Franz will be sorry to hear that."

"There really is a Franz?"

He nodded. "He's my secretary."

She looked at him for a moment. "Secretary to a prince who doesn't want the throne? You know, I have to say, I find that part of this pretty hard to believe as well."

"Why is that?"

"It defies human nature. People *want* to be royalty. They don't want to move *out* of the castle, they want to move *in*. It makes no sense for you to go searching for another heir—" A thought too horrible to voice came to her. Maybe he *did* want the throne. Maybe he wanted to find what he called the "legitimate heir" so he could get rid of any possible threat.

"What's the matter?" he asked, concern coming over his face. "Are you ill?"

Amy tried to regain her composure. If he did want to get rid of her, she mustn't appear to be afraid. "No, I'm fine," she said, but her voice was weak.

"No, you're not." He got up and went to the small refrigerator across the room. When he came back he had a bottle of cold water. "Perhaps this will help."

He was trying to help her. If he didn't care what happened to her—indeed, if he wished ill upon her— he wouldn't try to help her, would he?

She took the water. "Thank you."

"What happened to you?"

She shook her head. "It was nothing."

His gaze was penetrating. "I don't believe you."

She gave a dry laugh. "That makes us even."

He didn't share her levity. "You don't trust me," he said quietly. "And that scares you."

She was so shocked at his accurate assessment that her mouth dropped open. "I didn't say that!"

"You didn't have to."

"But—"

"It's all right. Were I you, I would be equally skeptical."

"It's not just skepticism."

He studied her for a moment. "Surely you don't believe I mean you harm."

"What makes you say that?"

"The look in your eyes." He leaned forward and put his hands on hers. "You're afraid of me."

"I'm not."

He watched her in silence before saying, "You don't believe I want to give up the throne. You said as much yourself. So this is…" He made an expansive gesture. "You believe I intend to, how do you say, get rid of the competition?"

She raised her chin and hoped he couldn't hear the nervous pounding of her heart. "That's an interesting theory."

He chuckled softly. "It's true, Americans watch too much television." His eyes met hers. "No, Amé, I do not want to eliminate you. I want you to take the throne, where you belong. But I will tell you the truth, it's not purely from a feeling of illegitimacy on my part."

Finally he was starting to be honest. She believed he didn't mean her harm. He'd gone to too much trouble to find her and tell her who he believed she was. Relieved, Amy asked, "What is it?"

"This is not something I wanted to share so soon," he said, standing up and going to the iced champagne. "But under the circumstances, I suppose I must."

"I'm listening."

He filled his glass and turned to face her. "Lufthania was once one of the wealthiest nations in Europe. Now there are people starving in the streets."

"Why?" Amy gasped. "What happened?"

"The laws regarding imports, and therefore exports, were tightened. People were no longer able to make a living creating Lufthania's greatest product."

"What is that?"

"Chocolate."

Chocolate! She was being taken to rule a country whose greatest product was chocolate! Her heart leapt. There was nothing he could have said that would have made her feel more like she belonged there. "And the people no longer make it?"

He shook his head grimly. "We are a democracy run by dictators." He gave a small shrug. "That is, much of the current regime disapproves of progress, of technology and thus of the way the rest of Europe and the world live. They would not let electronic imports in, which cut off a good deal of our export business and left many families unable to earn their living."

It was hard to believe. "Your government would rather see its people starve than move into the twenty-first century?"

"Exactly."

She believed him. There was no way a person could fake the disgust he showed for the situation. "And what does finding a new princess have to do with it? How can that help?"

"It can help," he said, "because by bringing a beautiful American princess in, a modern woman from a modern world who cannot be removed from the public eye by a vote or other means, the country can move forward."

"But how? What if they just hate me? Or whoever ends up on the throne," she corrected quickly.

He smiled and took a sip of his champagne. "You've seen this phenomenon over and over. A beautiful young royal enters the public eye and soon young girls everywhere are imitating her, demanding information about her from the press. It's the kind of thing the government is powerless to control."

"Like with Princess Diana."

"Precisely. And a handful of others." He gestured toward the magazine next to her. "That publication is one of many devoted exclusively to European royalty. But I am not as interesting to them as you will be."

She thought about the article on him, and the extremely good photographs of him. He was probably a heartthrob to thousands of women in his country. Millions, if there were that many.

"I doubt anyone would be more interesting than you to the media."

He tipped his glass toward her. "You are too kind."

But she was not to be distracted. "Okay, so I understand the theory behind this, though I'm not sure it's right to just pick anyone to take over and pretend to be the princess—"

"You *are* the princess."

She held a hand up. "Okay, say I am. What do you do when I take the throne?"

He hesitated.

"Will?"

He expelled a long breath. "I want to take a job in the government. The only way I can change things is from the inside. Not from a gilded perch designed only for the amusement of the old school."

"But if you're the crown prince, can't you make the laws and force the government to uphold them?"

"No, it is as I told you. The prince or princess is merely a figurehead. The throne holds no power."

"And a royal can't run for office."

"No."

Now she got it. Now it all made sense. And Will was a much better man than she'd given him credit for. His eagerness to find a replacement was not from laziness, or from the desire to do away with another heir so he could hold on to power forever, it was from his concern for his country.

His people.

For one wild moment, she wanted nothing more than to help him. No matter what it took. "I understand," she said. "And I admire you for it."

He smiled that dazzling smile. "Then you will help?"

"I—"

"Your Highness," a voice interrupted from the doorway.

They turned to see a large man in what must have been a captain's or co-captain's uniform.

"Yes, Max?"

The man spoke in German, which Amy didn't understand, and Will responded in the same language, before turning back to her. "We're landing in ten minutes," he said. "Put your seat belt on and look out the window. You're about to see your country."

Chapter Four

It was a long ten minutes for Will, waiting for the plane to land. But for once it wasn't because of his anxiety about flying.

This time it was because of the woman sitting in front of him.

Princess Amelia.

He couldn't believe he had been foolish enough to kiss her. It wasn't just that personal involvement wasn't part of his plan—personal involvement was something he was specifically determined to avoid with the new princess. It could jeopardize all of his plans.

Giving up his place on the throne of the country he had loved since birth wasn't an *easy* thing for Will. The palace alone would be hard to leave, perched atop a mountainside looking over the beautiful valley of

Lufthania—so green in summer, and glazed like a daz-zling gem with snow and ice in the winter. He would miss the view of the shadows cutting across the hills when he woke up every morning, and the lights of the village twinkling in the distance like stars when he went to bed at night.

But he would not miss the adoration and respect he felt he had not rightfully earned as prince. He would be far more comfortable working legitimately for the people than he was now.

So it would be with a heavy heart, but steely deter-mination, that he would pass the throne back to Ame-lia. However, if he made the mistake of getting in-volved with her personally—even as a friend—it would be even more difficult to leave palace life be-hind, because from now on that life would include Amelia.

He looked at her profile as she looked out the win-dow. Her nose was straight and just long enough to avoid being called pert. Her chin was strong yet del-icate, and her eyes were like clear blue glass. He couldn't read her expression as Lufthania came into full view, but he sensed her awe.

Who wouldn't feel awe upon seeing this lovely place for the first time? To this day, Will's chest filled with pride every time he saw it after a trip abroad. Only today, he felt more than that. Today he had a profound sense of coming home.

It was strange. When he'd imagined what it would be like to bring Amelia back, he'd thought he might feel some sense of loss or of intrusion. Yet she didn't raise any of those feelings in him.

In fact, as difficult as it was to believe, it was *she* who gave him this added sense of home this time. It was as if he was clicking the last missing piece into a puzzle and now it was complete.

"What do you think?" he asked her.

"I think I'm dreaming."

He gave a half smile. "If you are, I'm flattered to be part of it."

She laughed and shook her head. "I mean I think I'm dreaming of the scene outside, *not* of you."

"Give it time."

She looked at him.

"I mean, give Lufthania time," he said. "You will see that this is all real. And all yours."

"Did you ever think of being a used-car salesman?" she asked, unfazed as the plane bumped the ground and taxied rapidly down the runway. "Because I bet you could make a fortune."

"I'll keep it in mind."

The plane drew to a halt and Will unclipped his seat belt. This was his favorite part of any flight.

Annabelle opened the door and said, "Your car is waiting, sir."

He looked at Amy. "Are you ready?"

She bit her lower lip. "I'm not sure."

"Come on, then. Let me try to sell you a country..."

The road twisted and turned through a snow-white fairy-tale forest. And, as in most fairy tales, there was a slightly menacing undertone to the journey. Though the snow was bright, the woods were so thick they were dark in the distance. And the winding road had patches of ice that crackled under the tires of the sleek limousine.

Amy looked out the window and told herself she was crazy for imagining that the landscape was familiar. Yet she couldn't shake the feeling of having been here before.

"What are you thinking?" Will asked, his voice so low and so close to her ear that it sent chills down the back of her neck.

"That it's very beautiful here," she said, though that was only half the truth. "This is a nice vacation, if nothing else."

"If nothing else," he repeated. "You are not an easy one to persuade, are you, Amé?"

"Not without cold, hard facts," she said.

"Cold, hard?" He looked puzzled.

"It's an expression," she explained. "Basically it means I won't believe I'm a princess until you prove it." And that she was ready, in the meantime, to leave at a moment's notice, if necessary. She had her passport, her credit cards, and she could do without her luggage if necessary.

"The palace physician will test your blood tomorrow morning, if that suits you," he said. "It will be tested against your grandfather's, and you will have the proof you need within a couple of weeks." He raised an eyebrow. "I know you are expecting it to be negative, but have you considered what you must do if—*when*—it is positive? You'll be moving here immediately, I assume.''

She didn't answer right away. She honestly hadn't thought of what she'd do if the test proved she was related to the former prince and princess. The notion had been so fantastic that she couldn't take it seriously.

Now, faced with the question of what she'd do, she realized that she did have to plan for that possibility. Though the *idea* of being some kind of secret princess was hard to believe, the facts of her life didn't necessarily point against it. She had been in a car accident with her parents, two people who were never identified. And, apparently, never missed, at least in America, because the police department had put out a nationwide call for missing persons that yielded nothing. It was a sad thing that was better explained by Wilhelm's theory than by the idea that no one cared enough about them to miss them.

''Amé?''

She turned her attention back to Will. ''I don't know,'' she said honestly. ''If you're right... So much of my life is in America. My business, my friends, my parents, my apartment.'' She shrugged. ''My bills. Everything. How could I just abandon all of that?''

''Don't think of it as abandoning,'' he said. His green eyes were so warm he could have convinced her of almost anything. ''It is moving on, fulfilling your destiny. It is a great thing.''

Somehow, looking into those eyes and thinking of

destiny sent a thrill through Amy. Which, she told herself immediately, was foolish because he was not offering himself but his country. This was not a prince looking for a princess, it was a man looking for a replacement.

"Let's just see what the test results are," she said, turning her attention from his handsome face to the brushed-cotton landscape outside. "Then we'll discuss 'forever.'"

He leaned back against the seat and mused, "I believe that is the first time a woman has said *forever* to me without giving me a chill."

Amy turned and looked at him. "Should I be flattered?"

"Undoubtedly." The corner of his mouth twisted up into a half smile.

The car drew to a halt by a guard's station, and Will pushed the button to lower his window. "Gustav," he said to the middle-aged man inside. "She is here." He gestured toward Amy.

The guard did not look at her. "Yes, sir."

"I want security tightened to a maximum. No one enters the property without permission from myself or Franz, is that clear?"

"Yes, sir." The guard saluted without letting his eyes leave Will.

"Very good." Will closed his window and the driver continued on.

"Warm fellow," Amy commented.

Will gave a laugh. "He takes his job very seriously. He was my chauffeur until three weeks ago. Before that, he was my father's chauffeur. It's taken some time for him to work his way up to guard."

"I see." What she saw was that maybe the people here weren't going to be as warm to her arrival as Will was. She didn't want to be a wimp, but part of her suddenly felt homesick and insecure.

It was probably just the jet lag, she decided. She wasn't usually a nervous person. She loved adventure. And this, without a doubt, was the greatest adventure of her life so far.

She looked back out the window just as they rounded a hairpin turn and came into view of the most magnificent castle she'd ever seen.

"My God," she gasped. "Don't tell me that's—"

"Your new home," Will finished. "It is."

"But it's—when you said this was a small country...that the economy was so bad...I just assumed..." She was speechless.

He laughed. "You assumed what? That it would be a tent somewhere in the woods? Come now, Amé, Lufthania was once a grande dame. This castle has stood for centuries, hosting great nobility throughout the ages."

She could believe it. The castle was like a gingerbread confection painted with white icing. There were winding spires and tall turrets, and more windows than Amy could count. Despite the snowy, icy exterior, the windows glowed yellow and promised a warm refuge from the cold inside.

"Let them know we're here," Will said to the driver, then turned to Amy. "Do you like it?"

"It's breathtaking," she said honestly.

"Somehow I knew you'd feel that way." He smiled and pointed to the building. "You see that room way up at the top?"

"Yes."

"That was your nursery."

Sadness filled her suddenly. It was *someone's* nursery, anyway. Someone who was sent away, into the cold, in the dead of night.

She was spared having to answer when the car stopped in a snowless brick courtyard in front of a wide wooden door.

"Are you ready?" Will asked Amy.

Part of her wanted to scream "No! Take me home!" but she knew she had not yet finished what she'd come here to do. And if she turned away now—if she even could—she would wonder forever if, by some tiny chance, this really was where she belonged.

She nodded. "I'm ready."

He got out of the car and went around to let her out, dismissing the attempts of the chauffeur to open the door. He took her by the hand, then offered an arm to escort her in. She was grateful for it. He offered warmth and support and, strangely, a modicum of familiarity at the most intimidating moment of her life.

"The staff will be inside to greet you," he said quietly. "Don't worry that you need to make conversation. It is not expected. Just stand and smile as they introduce themselves."

She nodded mutely.

The doors opened and Will led her into an enormous marble entryway, with a wide, sweeping stair-case that put Tara's to shame and a chandelier that had to weigh at least a thousand pounds.

Lined up directly beneath it were about twenty-five black-and-white-uniformed staff members, all standing erect. No one made eye contact with Amy, and for a moment she feared that they resented her intrusion on the palace.

On Will's command, they introduced themselves one by one, meeting her eyes as they did. For the most part, their smiles seemed genuine and warm, and Amy's fears about being an interloper slowly dis-solved.

One older man, introduced as Christian, had been there when Princess Lily had fled and had been a faith-ful servant to her family. "You are the picture of your mother," he said, his voice wavering slightly.

Amy didn't know what to say. She didn't want to encourage the belief that she was Princess Lily's daughter for fear that everyone would be disappointed when the test results came back. "Thank you," she said sincerely. "That is a great compliment."

"Oh, thank you, ma'am."

"It will be nice to have Amé around, won't it?" Will gave the man a smile so kind that it made Amy's chest feel tight.

"It certainly will," Christian said. "It certainly will."

Finally, they got to the last person, a tall, broad woman with gray hair, who was weeping so hard she couldn't speak.

"This," Will said, laying a hand gently on the woman's shoulder, "is Letty. Leticia. She was your nanny."

Amy barely had time to process what he'd said before the woman came at her with open arms.

Amy fell into the older woman's embrace and had just a moment of startled confusion before the world went black. Though she later tried to tell herself it was only her jet lag catching up with her, the truth was that something else came over her: a familiarity so strong it overwhelmed her. She couldn't face it.

When she came to, Amy was on a fussy wooden sofa in what must have been some sort of formal reception room. Will was kneeling at her side, holding her hand in his and looking at her with grave concern, while Letty stood several feet away, kneading a white handkerchief in her hands and saying over and over, "Amé, my Amé."

"I'm sorry," Amy said, still groggy. She struggled to sit up. "I don't know what happened."

"It's been a difficult day," Will said, still holding her hand. "I asked too much of you."

"No, it's not that...." She put a hand to her forehead. "I'm just tired."

Letty heard her voice and came rushing over. "My darling, darling girl. Are you all right?"

Amy nodded.

The woman's face split into a wide smile. "Thank God. You are home at last, Amé. We have waited so long. So very long."

Amy took a sip of the water Will offered.

"We must take her to her room," Letty said to Will. "She must be made to feel at home right away. Clearly the girl needs her rest."

"Is her room ready?"

Letty nodded. "I made sure of it." She turned to Amy and gave a huge, apple-cheeked smile. "Would you like to go lie down in your old room? I've prepared it just the way your mother liked it."

"English," Will said to Letty. "She doesn't understand."

Letty shot him a puzzled look, then said to Amy, "Do you understand me, darling?"

Amy nodded, feeling like she was stepping out of a fog. "Sure."

Letty looked at Will, but he was staring down at Amy in disbelief. "I thought you didn't speak German."

"I don't."

"What do you mean? How were you able to answer Letty just now?"

Amy frowned. "I answered in English," she said, thinking it was a very strange and obvious thing to have to point out.

"Yes," he said patiently. "But Letty addressed you in German."

An hour later, when Amy had been installed in her suite and was under the watchful and adoring eye of Letty, Will went to his office to reassess the situation.

This was all more difficult than he had anticipated it would be. He had no doubt that she was Princess

Amelia—the large portfolio in front of him held more than enough proof of that. And if that wasn't enough proof, her inexplicable understanding of German, which she had said she didn't speak a word of, cemented Will's conviction.

What he hadn't anticipated was that she, herself, would be so difficult to convince. Finding her had seemed to be the hard part. It had taken years, scores of investigators and countless false leads before he'd finally found Amy.

Once he had, he'd been so relieved that it felt like the worst was over. He'd fully expected to be able to walk into her shop, tell her what he'd learned and carry her suitcases out to the car for her. When she'd asked for proof—''cold, hard facts'' as she'd say—he had been surprised but amused. The portfolio full of papers that he'd had translated into English—in case anyone did have questions—seemed to him more than adequate.

That it wasn't still baffled him. It was as if Amy was looking for an excuse *not* to be Amelia, rather than enjoying the fact that she had not only found her origins but that she was, indeed, a royal princess.

Over the years, Will had met more women than he cared to think about who would have given just about anything to be a princess. What was it about Amy that made her resist it?

Whatever it was, it intrigued Will.

He put the portfolio aside and was getting ready to leave his office when there was a knock at the door and his secretary, the real Franz Burgess, entered.

"Pardon me, sir," said the old man, who had been Will's father's secretary before him. "Has the lady been installed in her room?"

"She has." Will was careful not to give away too much information about Amé, as he wasn't sure where Franz stood on the matter of returning Amé's family to the throne.

Franz looked fretful for a moment, then closed the door behind him. "Might I have a word with you?"

Will sat down and gestured toward the seat before him. "Please."

Franz didn't sit but stood in front of the desk. "I have heard...rumblings," he said. "There are those who would prefer that she wasn't here."

Will leaned back in his chair and assessed Franz. "Are you one of them?"

Franz straightened his back. "It is not for me to decide it one way or the other."

Will hesitated. "Franz," he said steadily. "You know I believe her to be the rightful heir to the throne."

"I do, sir."

"I will not tolerate any disrespect toward her, do you understand?"

"Of course, sir."

Will raised an eyebrow. "And you will pass that word along to the rest of the staff, I trust?"

"Indeed, sir."

A very light knock at the door caught Will's attention and he looked at Franz. "Did you hear something?"

Franz nodded. "At the door." He strode across the room and opened the heavy oak door, revealing Amy standing there, looking very delicate with her long ginger hair pulled back and wearing a green silk dressing gown.

"I'm sorry to bother you," she said with an apologetic smile toward Will.

"No bother at all," he said, then, seeing her uncertain glance at Franz, said to the man, "That will be all, Franz. Thank you for your cooperation."

Franz put his heels together and gave a slight, stiff bow, then left the room.

Amy watched him go, then made a face. "They take you very seriously around here, don't they?"

He laughed. "And you find this hard to believe?"

Her face went pink. "Oh, no, no, I didn't mean that. I only meant…well, you're just so young and so…" Her face went from pink to red.

"So…?" he prompted, curious as to what else she thought of him.

She gazed at him for just a moment, before quickly looking away. "Where I come from no one gets that kind of deference." She shrugged. "Not even the president."

"You will get used to it."

She looked as if she was about to object—and he knew already what her objection would be, that she didn't know if she would be staying—but she stopped and gave him a look that made his heart trip. "You are persistent, aren't you?"

"It's one of my finer traits."

"Along with modesty."

"Ah, I have more of that than most." He wanted to go to her and take her in his arms. She looked so lovely in the infernally inadequate light of the castle that it took his breath away. "Why did you come to see me?"

"It's a little embarrassing, actually," she said. "I was trying to make a phone call from my room, but I couldn't get my cell phone to work. Is there some code I should dial for an outside line on one of the palace phones?"

"No, you can dial directly."

She splayed her arms. "There's no dial tone at all."

Most likely it was a loose wire. The castle had plenty of those, as well. He would be able to fix it easily, but he was reluctant to go to her room with her. He didn't trust himself, and this was no time for him to get close to her.

And she was absolutely the wrong person to start a relationship with.

"I'll have someone go up and take care of it for you," he said. "Sometimes the wires need to be manipulated, that's all."

She glanced at her watch, looked fretful and said, "Thank you." She turned to go but he stopped her.

"Wait, Amé."

She turned back around. "What?"

"Why do you look so worried?"

She gave a brief smile. "Because I've never been able to disguise my feelings." She shook her head. "I'm just anxious to call my parents. With all the excitement when I arrived, I forgot all about it, and I'm sure they're just insane with worry. Maybe there's another phone I could use?''

''Absolutely.'' He went to his phone and lifted the receiver toward her. ''Please. Take your time. And I'll go up and see if I can fix the one in your room.''

He had heard the expression about twinkling eyes before, but he'd never actually *seen* what it meant until now.

''Quite a handy prince, aren't you?'' she joked.

''I could send someone up, if you prefer,'' he said, his voice stiffer than he had intended. ''But it could take a while.''

She put her hand on his arm. ''I'm sorry, I didn't mean that I wanted someone else to do it instead. It's just that…well…you're the *prince*. I can't believe you can do telephone repairs.''

Her touch was warm against his skin. He looked from her hand to her eyes, irritated at how disconcerted she made him feel. ''I studied engineering at university,'' he explained, even though he knew she wasn't seriously asking for his qualifications.

''Boy, I wish you could come back to my apartment with me,'' she said.

''I beg your pardon?''

''The wiring there is really funky. I can't turn on the coffeemaker without turning off the television first. It drives me nuts.''

''Then you should stay here. You'll never have to worry about your coffeemaker again.'' He smiled. ''But the telephones don't always work.''

She smiled back and shrugged. "It's always something, I guess."

"I'll leave you to your call now," he said. "And I'll see you tomorrow. In the meantime, if you have any problems, call on Letty or Christian."

"I will, thanks."

He left her and hurried to her room so he could fix the problem and leave before she got back.

He should have called on one of the palace engineers, he knew that. It probably wouldn't have taken them longer than fifteen minutes to get to the phone. But he didn't want a stranger going to Amé's room. It was probably sheer paranoia on his part, but after what Franz had told him, he wanted to be absolutely sure that everyone who had close contact with her had her best interests at heart.

Like Letty and Christian.

And himself.

When he reached her room and pushed open the door, instead of the silence of what should have been an empty room, there was a startled exclamation from the other side of her bed.

Chapter Five

"Who's there?" Will asked, striding angrily across the floor.

"It's me, sir." Christian rose from the floor behind the bed, his hands behind his back.

Will stopped. "What on earth are you doing there?"

"Princess Amé's telephone..." Christian gestured toward the table with one arm. "It wasn't working. I was, er, trying to repair it."

"I see." Will approached him. "And did you?"

Christian shook his head and produced his other hand, and in it a wire. "I'm afraid I only made things worse."

Will stifled an oath, knowing that the old man was only trying to help. "I'll take care of it, Christian."

"I do apologize, sir."

The door burst open and Letty flew in, singing,

"Christian, did you—" She stopped short when she saw Will. "Good evening, sir." She dropped into a curtsey.

"Did I fix the telephone?" Christian asked, his voice louder than necessary. "I'm afraid I wasn't able to. But His Highness is going to."

She looked pleased. "How wonderful!"

"We should get out of his way," Christian said to her. "Unless there's anything else you need?" he asked Will.

"Nothing."

The two bustled out of the room, leaving Will alone. He didn't wonder at their strange behavior. After so many years of knowing them, he was used to it. They were the best of friends and, at times, cohorts. But everything they did, however misguided, came from their big hearts.

Like the time Will's fiancée, Ella, was lost in a skiing accident. He had spent months plunged in a deep depression, blaming himself for the accident. If he had only chosen a different day, a different mountain, if he'd stayed on the easier slopes with her instead of agreeing to meet at the lodge later, if...if...if... There were a million of them, a million ways in which her death was his fault.

Letty and Christian had tried everything to cheer him up, even going so far as to stage an "accident" in which Will could "save" Letty. They had set up a ladder by the door to the kitchen right about the time Will came in for his morning coffee. Letty had perched on top of the ladder, waiting for Will to come through the door, when she would ''fall'' off the ladder and into his arms, saving her from certain death. Or at least harm.

Unfortunately for them, Christian had forgotten something in the kitchen and, failing to warn Letty, had been the next one through the door instead of Will. Letty had fallen on the poor hapless old man, and they had both required a doctor's attention.

Yet in an odd way, their plan had succeeded in bringing Will out of his stupor. He'd realized that any man who had friends so loyal was lucky, and any ruler with subjects so loyal had a duty to serve them.

And that was when it had first occurred to him that he could better serve Letty and Christian—and thousands of others—as a civil servant and not as the royal figurehead.

This, he decided, would be his purpose in life. He wasn't destined to be a husband or a father. Perhaps he didn't deserve such precious responsibilities. But he could use whatever power he had left in his body and mind to help his fellow countrymen. Maybe—just maybe—he could make a positive difference for others.

So he'd immediately set about trying to find Princess Lily. Several months of research had led him to the sad fact of her death, but it wasn't long after that that he had managed to find her daughter. Amé. Amé.

He'd thought it would be easy. Just sweep into town, tell this fortunate young woman that she had won the ultimate lottery—that she was the rightful heir to the throne of Lufthania—and take her back to a joyful nation, where he could step out of the limelight.

He hadn't planned on her being so suspicious. Well, to be fair, it wasn't that she was suspicious so much as she was intelligent. And honest. A less honest person might have taken the crown regardless of whether or not she believed she deserved it. But not Amy Scott.

It was one of the things he really admired about her.

Which led to another problem. He hadn't planned on admiring her so much. He hadn't planned on having any personal feelings for her whatsoever. She was young, for heaven's sake, a good ten years younger than he was. And she was bullheaded. Not sweet and acquiescent, as Ella had been. As all the women he'd dated had been. Amé challenged almost everything he said. That would make him crazy very fast if they had a relationship.

But they weren't going to have a relationship. Not of any kind. Just a cordial acquaintance. Perhaps the occasional meeting when she began her reign, just so he could help her transition smoothly into her role.

In fact, he thought, kneeling down to the phone jack to repair the wire Christian had broken, he wasn't even going to do that much unless she asked for his help specifically. She would have plenty of advisers telling her what to do if she needed help.

He twisted the wires together and made a mental note to send someone up with electrical tape to finish the job. There was no need for him to come back to her bedroom, especially not tonight.

He lifted the receiver. The answering tone told him

his job was done, so he bent back down and used a pocket penknife to screw the jack back on. He was just finishing up when he heard the door open and Amy, presumably, came in, humming "Edelweiss."

"The telephone is working now," he said, standing up just in time to see Amy's back as she draped her dressing gown across the wing chair by the closet.

Amy whirled around, clapping her hands across her nightgown-covered chest.

"I'm sorry," he said, approaching her with his arms outstretched.

"What are you *doing?*" She stepped back.

"Getting this." He took her dressing gown from the chair and quickly draped it over her shoulders. "I didn't mean to startle you."

"Oh, my God." She put her hands over her face. He was horrified to see that her shoulders shook with what must have been terrible sobs.

"I'm so sorry." Gingerly, he put his hand on her shoulder, then took it off, thinking if he was the problem, then touching her could only make it worse.

She looked up at him, tears streaming from her eyes.

Guilt clenched his stomach. He had never had this particular effect on a woman, and he had no idea what to do. Should he leave? Stay and try to make it better? Call for a chaperone?

"Amé, I assure you, I wasn't going to..." He searched for the words. "Make an advance on you."

"I know." She wiped the tears from her cheeks and he realized, suddenly, that she was laughing. "You should have seen the look on your face.'' She dissolved into laughter again.

''The look on my face?''

She nodded. ''You startled me, and I guess I startled you. You looked like I'd caught you with your pants down.'' She wiped her cheeks again. ''I'm sorry, I must be punchy from jet lag.''

He didn't know what to say.

For the first time in his life, he didn't know what to say.

She straightened her back and put on a serious face. ''I guess it isn't proper to tell a prince he looks like he's been caught with his pants down.''

''It isn't something I've heard before,'' he said carefully.

She smiled. ''It's just an expression. And one more illustration of what a terrible princess I'd make for your country.''

''I don't know. People might find you refreshing.''

She tightened the sash of the dressing gown. ''That's a nice way of putting it.''

''I mean it.'' He caught her gaze and held it. ''I find you refreshing myself.''

She blinked. ''You do?''

He nodded and resisted the urge to touch her. ''Very much so.'' The air around them suddenly felt thick. One more moment of looking down into her blue eyes and he wouldn't be able to stop himself from kissing her. Again. He stepped back. ''As I said, your telephone is working now. Were you able to contact your parents?''

She pushed her hands into the pockets of her gown and took a step away herself. "Yes, I was. Fortunately, they'd figured my first hours here would be busy, so they weren't too worried."

"Good."

Silence shuddered between them.

"Then I'll see you in the morning," he said.

"Great."

"The doctor will be here to administer the blood test directly after breakfast."

She nodded. "Fine."

He nodded, too. "So I'll see you then."

"Okay. Good night."

"Good night." He let himself out the door and closed it behind him, then stopped in the hall. When had he become such a stumbling idiot? Something about Amy made him as nervous as a young boy with a crush.

Maybe it was the fact that she was so much more outspoken than the women he'd known. One wrong move on his part and she would call him on it. No one had ever done that before.

As for her candid way of speaking to him...well, he'd told the truth about that. It *was* refreshing. All of his life, people had either pandered to him because he was the prince, or they'd cowered before him because he was the son of those who had taken over the throne. There didn't seem to be anyone who would just treat him like the man that he was. Even Ella had been eager to please him, even at the expense, he thought, of her own desires.

That was one of the reasons he'd felt so guilty about her death. She wasn't a very good skier, and he suspected she didn't like the sport even though she wouldn't admit it. When he'd tried to tell her it was all right that she didn't share that hobby with him, she'd insisted that she wanted to, and she'd come along on the trip.

He shook the memory from his mind. It didn't bear thinking about now. He'd learned from his mistake, that was enough. Whether it was his personality or his position that caused the problems, there would be no women in his future. At least not long-term relationships with women, he conceded, granting that occasionally one *did* need warm companionship on a cold night.

He would *not* fall in love.

Especially—he couldn't help the thought—with a forthright, fearless, bright-eyed American who was taking over his role on the throne.

His family had conquered hers a quarter of a century ago, and he would make right that wrong. But he would not let her conquer his heart in return.

Amy lay on the plush feather bed, blinking in the darkness. The cotton sheets were as soft as satin, the down comforter thick and warm, yet she shivered through the night.

At first she told herself it was jet lag. She'd been awake for a long time and had gone from the comfort of home this morning to a new country and culture this evening. It was hard to process all at once, that was all.

But now, as she lay in the luxury of a royal bed, she knew that *wasn't* all there was to it. There was something both sweet and haunting about this place. She felt at home. Yet something was missing.

Maybe it was just the arching rooms and long, echoing halls that made her feel that way. She thought of Will, living here all alone. Well, that wasn't entirely true, of course. There was a healthy-size staff living on the premises, but that wasn't the same as having your own family with you.

He must be lonely, Amy thought, with sudden compassion.

Or maybe he liked it that way. After all, he was a good-looking man. One might even say he was a *great*-looking man. Obviously he could have his choice of women. Yet for some reason he had, one could only assume, *chosen* to remain alone, apart from several meaningless dalliances that the magazine article she'd read had referred to.

He wasn't an easy man to figure out. And, really, there was no point in her trying until she knew whether or not she was going to be staying for longer than the brief amount of time it took to conduct the test.

When he'd first approached her with his story, she'd found it unbelievable. Even now she felt silly trying to think of herself as a princess. But his evidence had been fairly strong. More than that, when she'd looked at the picture of Princess Lily and seen the resemblance, she'd been shocked.

Then again, Will might have seen the photograph of Amy in the newspaper, noticed the resemblance himself, and drawn his conclusions from there, letting the evidence fall into place as it suited him. There were plenty of people in the world who bore a striking similarity to one another without being related at all.

Until she got the test results, Amy felt she had to protect herself from the hope of having found her family by reminding herself of that. She should just enjoy this strange, magical journey for what it was, she told herself repeatedly.

Just in case the clock struck midnight soon and it all ended.

She woke in the morning to Letty entering the room with a breakfast tray. The scent of strong coffee wafted across to Amy, and she sat up. "What time is it?"

"After ten, my dear." Letty set the tray down on the table by the bed. "I didn't want to wake you, but the doctor will be here in an hour."

"After *ten?*" Amy looked at her watch in disbelief. "I can't believe it."

"You had a long day yesterday, dear." Letty poured coffee out of a silver pot into a thin china cup. "Do you take cream and sugar?"

"Just cream, thanks." Amy pushed her hair back off of her forehead and tried to get her bearings.

"Just like your mother." Letty chuckled. "She

didn't like sweets. Except for chocolate. She loved my hot chocolate.'' She handed Amy the cup.

She took it and sipped the full-bodied coffee. It was delicious.

''It snowed again overnight,'' Letty was saying in thickly accented English, as she put a croissant on a plate along with a small dish of butter and raspberry preserves. ''It's quite lovely out. Shall I open the drapes?''

''Sure,'' Amy said, taking the plate from Letty. ''Thanks a lot.'' She ripped the croissant in half and smeared butter and preserves onto it. When she bit into it, the whole thing seemed to just melt in her mouth. ''Wow, this is great.''

''Annabelle made it,'' Letty said, drawing back the heavy drapery. The sun came streaming through the crystal-clear window, bringing the beautiful dusty-pink-and-gold room to life. ''She's the prince's favorite pastry chef.''

Amy paused with her coffee cup halfway to her lips. ''He mentioned that on the plane,'' she said, sounding more prim than she'd intended.

Letty turned to her with laughter in her eyes. ''There is nothing more to it than that.''

''It's none of my business.'' She sipped her coffee again, and tried to swallow the pride that kept her from asking Letty if the prince did have a girlfriend. It was just idle curiosity, and truly was none of her business, except that he *had* kissed her. If he'd done it while he had a girlfriend, that really made him a rat. But if she asked him about it…well, it was probably best to keep her mouth shut instead of inviting speculations about her own feelings for Will.

"Shall I get your clothes for you?" Letty asked, going to the walk-in closet.

"I haven't even unpacked yet." Amy threw back the sheets and got out of bed. "Everything was so crazy last night I didn't have time."

"I took care of that for you, dear." Letty came out of the closet holding Amy's denim dress. "How about this?"

"That's fine. Thanks so much for unpacking for me." Amy wasn't used to that kind of service. In truth it made her a little uncomfortable. "You really didn't need to do that."

Letty gave her a knowing smile. "Anything to make you more comfortable."

The woman looked so pleased with herself that Amy didn't know how to tell her that service like that made her uncomfortable, so instead she just smiled.

"Have you thought about what you'll wear to the ball?" Letty asked.

"I beg your pardon?" She must have misheard.

"The annual winter ball next Saturday evening," Letty explained. "Surely Prince Wilhelm told you about it."

"No." A winter ball. In the castle. This really was a fairy tale. "I don't think I'm included in the guest list."

Letty laughed. "The princess not included in the guest list? Indeed you are not, my dear. You are the hostess."

Amy's jaw dropped. "The *hostess!*"

"But of course!" Letty splayed her arms. "You are the princess."

"Well, no, Letty, we don't know that." She didn't mean to sound cold. "In fact, I don't think I believe it. I wish you wouldn't get your hopes up."

Letty stepped back, looking appalled. "You don't believe that Princess Lily is your mama? Surely you don't mean it."

"I'm sorry, but—"

"Have you not looked in the mirror, child? Do you not see the likeness?"

"I suppose there is some likeness, but—"

"More than *some,* dear. You are her image." Letty came over to her and pulled her into a warm embrace. "Besides that, I would know you anywhere. I held you as a babe, and cared for you as I did your mother before you. I would have known you anywhere."

She looked so sincere that Amy didn't have the heart to disagree with her. Instead, she said, "We'll have the test results soon enough."

Letty gave her a skeptical look. "It breaks my heart that you cannot remember your time here, or your dear mother. But I suppose it's to be expected. You were such a small thing when they took you away."

A lump formed in Amy's throat. "It was a long time ago," she agreed noncommittally. Then, to change the subject, she added, "I should get downstairs so I'm ready when the doctor arrives."

"Indeed," Letty agreed, holding the dress out to her.

Amy took it and stepped into it, modestly removing

her nightgown when the other dress was covering her. She buttoned the front and stepped over to the mirror to straighten her hair.

Letty appeared behind her and touched her hair. "You are her image," she said, for the second time. "There is no doubt. Welcome home, Amé. It has been far too long."

Amy was so moved by the look in the older woman's eyes that she turned around and impulsively gave her a hug. "Princess Lily was lucky to have you, Letty," she said. "You must have been a great comfort to her."

"Not enough, I'm afraid," Letty said ruefully. Then her expression changed. "But everything will return to normal now. It will be exactly as it should be." She gave a wide smile. "Are you ready?"

"I just need my shoes."

"Oh! They are here!" Letty hurried to the closet and returned with the shoes that Amy always wore with this particular dress.

She didn't even bother to ask how Letty had known. She simply put the shoes on and followed the older woman through the long hallways and down the cold, wide stairways to the reception room on the first floor.

The first person she noticed in the room was Will. He wore a dark sweater and faded blue jeans, and looked more like a construction worker on the weekend than a prince, which made him all the more appealing.

Okay, she granted, maybe *appealing* was just a little bit of an understatement. The truth was that she had already seen the regal side of him, the proud prince who commanded the attention and respect of those around him. This rugged boy-next-door look took her by surprise and drew her to him even more.

Amy was astonished at her feelings upon seeing him. Everything that was happening around her was confusing, but just seeing him lifted her above the fray. It was as if all the noise and frenzy receded into the background and they were the only ones in the room. The memory of their kiss on the plane came back to her in full technicolor.

Did he think about it, too?

She pushed the thought from her mind. This was silly. She was transferring all kinds of feelings to Will because she was a stranger in a foreign land, going through a process that could change her whole life. It made sense that she looked to the one person here that she'd known—or met, anyway—back home as an island in a vast sea.

Will was just her island.

And psychologically, she viewed him as her way out if things got to be too much, although realistically she knew darn well she could call an airline and get a flight out herself.

As soon as he saw her, his eyes lit up and he came over to her.

Her heart pounded with every one of his strides.

"Good morning, Amé. Did you sleep well?"

"Extremely well," she said, trying to sound nonchalant. "It was almost like I was tranquilized."

He frowned for a moment, then said, "You must have been exhausted."

"I was." A chill ran over her and she rubbed her hands along her arms. "So, is one of these men the doctor?"

"Yes. Dr. Trilling," he called, and a very tall man with gray hair turned to them.

When he saw who had summoned him, the doctor came over to Will and Amy. "Your Highness?"

"Doctor, this is Amy Scott," Will said, gesturing toward Amy.

She was grateful that he didn't introduce her as the princess. "Hi," she said, taking the hand the doctor proffered.

"It's a pleasure to meet you," Dr. Trilling said, bowing. "I've heard so much about you already."

She glanced uncertainly at Will, who said, "Word travels fast."

"I'll say."

"Are you ready for the test?" the doctor asked. "It will only take a moment and I'd like to get the sample to the laboratory as soon as possible."

"I'm all for that," Amy said, acutely aware of Will's eyes on her. "Where do you want me to go?"

The doctor showed her to a chair and asked her to push her sleeve up.

Will stood nearby and looked on. "This won't hurt," he assured her.

"I've given blood before," she said with a smile, touched by his unnecessary reassurance. "Don't worry about me—ouch!"

"I apologize," the doctor said, loosening the rubber tie on her upper arm. "Sometimes it pinches a bit."

She gave Will a look and he shrugged.

She turned back to look at the vial filling rapidly with her future. So much depended on the blood within. So many questions could be answered, if only Will's theory was correct. The vial filled quickly and before she knew it, he had removed the needle and placed a bandage over the spot.

"That's all we need," the doctor said, handing the vial to another man, who wrote Amy's name on it. "I'll rush the results as much as I can."

"Very good," Will said.

Amy watched as the doctor and his small entourage quickly gathered their things and left. When they had, the room felt nearly empty.

"That's a lot of people for just one blood test," she remarked to Will.

"There are a lot of people who want to ensure that the test results are accurate," he answered. "That should put your mind somewhat at ease."

She laughed. "I don't know *what* could put my mind at ease at this point."

"I hope the truth will." He looked so deeply into her eyes, she felt naked. "I hope your birthright will bring you the peace you seek."

She wanted so badly to believe it, but caution welled in her. "Will, you don't seem to be allowing for even the *possibility* that you're wrong about who I am," she said, concerned. "I *hope* you're right, I truly do, but you may be in for a big surprise."

"You have surprised me more than once already," he said, cocking his head to the side. "I have no doubt you will surprise me again. But this test will not. I already know who you are. And I hope you will be able to accept it when the results come back."

Chapter Six

Their conversation was interrupted by Christian. "May I have a word with you, sir?" he asked, then, with an apologetic nod at Amy, added, "A private word?"

"Excuse me," Amy said quickly. "I think I saw some orange juice on the table over there, I'll just go and get a glass. You gentlemen take your time."

Will watched her go, then turned back to Christian, who looked very serious.

Amy watched them from across the room, marveling at how conspicuously good-looking Will really was. He was the perfect Prince Charming, tall and graceful, and so handsome it made her ache sometimes. On top of that, he was truly noble, looking out for Amy's well-being.

He returned to her and explained, "Christian and

Letty are most concerned about the fact that you do not plan to attend the winter ball. I believe they have Cinderella visions for you.''

She smiled. ''That's sweet, but I didn't even *know* about the winter ball until this morning. And it's just a week away. By then I may be gone.''

He shook his head, giving a light smile. ''And by then you may be, officially, Princess Amelia of Lufthania. In which case, your presence at the ball would be expected.''

''I hate to keep harping on this, but my presence at the bookshop is also expected.'' Okay, the truth was that she would far prefer to be at a ball in an Alpine palace, but she was fairly certain that the test results would have sent her packing by then. ''Don't forget I have a life to get back to.''

''A life that could easily be handled from here, if you chose to retain the bookshop after you are crowned.'' He took a step closer to her.

Suddenly, it was as if everyone in the room faded into the background. There was no one there except the two of them.

''Is there something else in your life in the United States that truly compels you to return?''

Her face felt warm. ''My *life* compels me to return.'' She knew she should step away from him, but she didn't.

''What in particular?'' He looked into her eyes. ''Your parents? They can easily be brought here. The store? Your employee? The nights you spend alone in your apartment?''

"You don't know anything about my private life." She stepped back quickly. "And you have no right to imply that it's meaningless."

"I didn't say it was meaningless."

"You might as well have." She looked fiercely into his eyes. "Listen, *Your Highness,* I may not be some snooty royal, featured monthly in tabloid magazines, but my life is every bit as worthwhile as yours is."

"Perhaps more so," he said quietly, unruffled by her outburst. "You've misunderstood me. It isn't the value of your life that is in question, it's where it's best for you to spend it. I've no doubt that you make the lives of your customers and employee more pleasant in your dealings with them. You are no doubt as important to them as they are to you, but you have the opportunity to make a difference to an entire nation. A small one to be sure..." He nodded. "But a nation nevertheless."

"There are hundreds, probably *thousands,* of people who could do that better than I could." Amy was close to tears, but she didn't want him to see that.

"That," he said, touching her cheek, "is not true. No one else represents what you do. No one else *is* Lufthania, as you are."

She looked at him wordlessly.

"Tell me," he said after a moment. "Is there someone in particular whom you wish to return to?" He hesitated. "A man?"

His question caught her off guard. "Didn't your research answer that for you?"

"My research was incomplete in that area."

Not as incomplete as her life had been, she'd wager. "What is it you want to know?" she asked, heart pounding.

There wasn't much to say. In twenty-eight years, she'd had one serious boyfriend—also known as her one serious mistake—in college. It had taken a conscious effort, but she had learned to trust him...right before he'd left her for her roommate. He'd called Amy emotionally inaccessible, which she took as code for cold.

Since then, there had been no serious boyfriends at all. She didn't want to let anyone in.

"I want to know," Will said, "if there's someone special you want to return to in the States." He hesitated before adding, "Someone special whom we should perhaps arrange to come here?"

She gave a dry laugh. No, there was no one special to return to. No one who would particularly miss her. Not even a cat. "Why do you want to know that?" she asked, though she found herself nervous about his answer. But whether or not she was nervous that he cared or he didn't care she didn't know.

He looked down for a moment, before answering, "It could affect your feelings about staying or not staying in Lufthania."

"My decision is my own," she contended. "It's not based on anyone else." *Not even you,* she added silently. It would be so easy to stay on in order to try to get to know Will better. It would be easy to accept his story and take on the glory of a title and remain in Lufthania close to him.

But she wouldn't let herself fall into that trap. She had made the mistake of falling hard for a man only once before in her life, and it had caused her enormous pain. She would *not* make that mistake again. She never wanted to feel that bereft again.

"I'm going to my room," she said.

"Wait—" he began.

"What?"

There was a long hesitation before he shook his head and said, "Nothing."

She wondered what he had wanted to say, but pride prevented her from asking. Instead she simply said, "Okay," and left the room, feeling his eyes on her every step of the way.

Several hours later, she was in her sitting room sending an e-mail to Mara to ask how business was going and to tell her about her adventure so far when Will showed up.

"Can you spare a moment?" he asked.

"That depends," she said. "Are you going to tell me my life at home is worthless again?"

He shook his head. "I didn't mean to say or imply that. My passion for this country and for your place in it made me speak too frankly. Or too enthusiastically. I do realize that you have quite a successful life in the United States. But what I know, and you don't yet, is that you were born into a great family here in Lufthania. You were born to the position of princess, and that is, or at least *was,* meant to be your destiny. When I think about the possibility of you *not* pursuing that destiny, it saddens me deeply."

"If I am who you say I am, I will take that responsibility into consideration, I promise you," she said.

"I appreciate that." He reached into his pocket. "I brought something for you. Call it a peace offering, if you like." He handed her what appeared to be a candy bar.

She frowned and tried to read the label, but it was in German. She spotted the word *schokolade*. "Chocolate?" she asked Will.

He nodded. "Try it."

She unwrapped the gold foil, broke off a piece and popped it into her mouth. It melted on her tongue like butter, filling her mouth with the most intense, rich chocolate flavor she had ever tasted. Her eyes widened. "This is amazing," she said.

"It's very good," he agreed.

"You could make a fortune selling this in the United States."

He splayed his arms. "Exactly. But right now we have small chocolatiers making this in tiny batches because it can only be sold in Lufthania. The only reason they can make a living at it at all is because the reputation for the chocolate's excellence has spread far and wide, and people cross the border to buy it in large quantities. Unfortunately, it's not in quantities large enough to sustain the economy."

"Is it legal to take food across the border like that?"

He smiled. "That's another problem. It costs a lot to declare a trunkful of chocolate."

"I see." She broke off another piece and put it in her mouth. Honestly, it not only gave her taste buds a lift but her mood as well. "This is something you hope to change?" She smiled. "Because that's a cause I can really get behind."

"I know it sounds frivolous, but, believe me, to the people of this country, it could make a world of difference to their quality of life."

She sobered. "I wish I could help."

"You will. Just by being here. Lufthania is undergoing a whole new revolution. A wonderful one. And it's thanks to you."

Her face grew warm. "I don't know about *that*."

He studied her for a moment, then asked, "Would you like to see the town?"

"When?"

"Right now. Why don't we take the car down so I can show you around. I think you'll find it quite charming."

"Well, gee, I had planned on sitting around doing nothing for a few more hours, but I suppose I can take a little time off."

He smiled. "Get a coat. I'll get the car and meet you in the front courtyard."

"Great."

They went their separate ways and Amy retrieved her coat from Letty, who had stashed it away heaven knows where, probably with the hopes that if Amy didn't have her coat, she wouldn't leave. Ever. It took some persuading for Letty to get it, but when she heard that Will was going to show Amy around, she jumped to the task eagerly.

Ten minutes later, Christian opened the door to a

crystal-white wonderland and Amy stepped outside into the lightly falling snow.

There was a low rumbling to the east and she looked over and saw a small SUV coming through the snow. When it got closer, she saw that Will was driving. No chauffeur, no security, just the man himself.

They would be alone.

A small, but hesitant thrill rushed through her as she went for the door. She barely reached the handle before he was there, opening it for her.

"Letty would have my head if I forced you into the indignity of having to open your own door," he explained with a smile. "She is one of the old school, very proper about things like this. She's probably watching us right now."

Amy had the feeling she was, but more because of her enthusiasm when she heard Amy would be going with Will than her suspicion that he might be anything less than a perfect gentleman.

Amy sat back against the soft leather seats and drank in the smell of crisp snow mingled with cold leather. It was enticing. Her spirits danced as he got in and asked, "Should we take the scenic route?"

"By all means!"

They laughed as he took off driving through the snow-covered hills, going off the larger road and onto a winding path through the woods and down the valley. As the snowflakes swirled dizzily in front of the windshield, Amy thought of the song "Winter Wonderland." There was no dirty, black street-side snow here, just piles of soft white cotton. It was absolutely lovely.

When Will rounded the last bend, the town center came into view in all its gingerbread-house glory. Though it was only late afternoon, the valley grew dark early and the shop lights were already on, casting warm, golden glows on the snow and the sidewalks.

Will drew the car up in front of—what else?—a chocolate shop.

"Is this another attempt to persuade me?" Amy asked.

"Perhaps."

"If this keeps up I'll weigh five hundred pounds."

He gave a rakish grin. "But you'll be beautiful, anyway."

"Wow. You're really good at this."

He shook his head. "I am completely sincere." He opened the door and walked around to open hers.

"Are you this sweet-talking with all the girls you try to hire as princesses?"

He met her eyes as he reached his hand forward to assist her from the car. "Only you, Amé. There is only you."

She caught herself before she went so far as to swoon, but she could have. She knew her cheeks had turned red, so she tried to cover for that by saying, "It certainly is brisk out here."

"Let's get inside, then," he said, opening his coat to cocoon her.

If she'd hoped to regain her composure, she failed

miserably. Powerless to refuse, she moved close to his body. For just a moment, she closed her eyes and took in the details of him: his clean, masculine scent, the penetrating warmth of his body, and the feel of his powerfully muscled chest against her arm. The closeness made her knees feel so weak she actually tripped in the snow.

His reflexes were quick, and he caught her with one powerful arm and held her close until they got to the door.

She wished the walk could have been a little bit longer.

When he stepped back to open the door for her, she felt cold where he had been. She wanted to ask him to come back and warm her up, but the gust of warmth that came from inside the shop told her that would be foolish. She walked over the threshold and he followed.

"Guten abend, Herr Baten," he called to the proprietor.

The man looked up lazily, caught sight of his patron and jumped to his feet. *"Guten abend, souverän."*

"My friend speaks only English," Will said, extending his arm toward Amy.

"Ah, good evening, madam," Herr George said to her.

"Good evening."

"Amy Scott, this is Herr George, who has owned this shop for nearly fifty years. Herr George, this is Amy Scott, a friend from America."

Herr George put his fingers to his lips. "But you know who she resembles...."

"Indeed," Will agreed, then changed the subject in order to avoid questions. "Do you have any of the chocolates you created for Princess Lily?"

"They are very popular." The old man looked through the glass display shelves until his eyes alighted on something. "There! One left!" He opened the back of the case and took out a small round light chocolate. "It is milk chocolate with butter cream and milk-chocolate cream combined inside." He handed it to Amy. "I created it for Princess Lily forty-five years ago because those were her favorite flavors. Go on. Try it."

Amy bit into the truffle and was immediately in love. The creams inside swirled in her mouth like a thick, sweet, warm drink. She closed her eyes and enjoyed the flavors, then said to Will. "Remember what I said about weighing five hundred pounds? It's a certainty. I want a hundred boxes of these." She looked at Herr George. "Honestly, this is the best thing I've ever tasted."

The man laughed just like Santa Claus. "This is quite a special young lady," he said to Will. "I hope you intend to keep her around for a while."

"I hope to," Will said, then put an arm around Amy's shoulder. "Come on. Let's look around a little more before night falls and the shops close. *Gute nacht,* Herr George."

The man raised a hand to them and said, *"Gute nacht."*

They stepped out into the night air, but this time Amy was so warmed by the experience that the cold didn't bother her so much. Not that she would have objected to being snuggled against Will again, but short of burrowing in herself, she didn't see how that was going to happen.

Next he took her to a clockmaker, a younger woman, perhaps mid-forties, who didn't seem to recognize Will or think Amy looked like anyone other than a customer. When he saw how captivated Amy was by a miniature cuckoo clock, he bought it for her on the spot, despite Amy's objections.

It was the same when she admired a watch in the jewelry shop, so she made a point of not saying a word about the beautiful sapphire ring in the front display case. But its workmanship was like nothing she'd ever seen before, and she kept on thinking how much the world was missing out on by not being able to import the works of these wonderful artisans.

By the time they went back to the car, Amy was weighed down with several bags of various wares from the shops, and the strange sensation of three people commenting on her likeness to Princess Lily.

When they were alone in the car, Will made it four. "You do look like her, you know."

"Princess Lily?"

"Your mother, yes." He drove forward through the night, lurching over snowdrifts and up the mountain, seemingly into the clouds.

"If I didn't know better, I'd say you hired them to say those things."

"There was no need."

They drove in silence for several minutes.

"What was it like growing up here?" Amy asked, looking out the window at the shapeless night.

"You imagine it was ideal, I suppose," he said. "A boy in a fairy-tale castle, but it was…different."

"How so?"

"You have to understand that my family was not welcomed by the people. They came to power through a hostile overthrow."

"Of which you didn't approve."

"Of which I understood very little," he corrected her. "I was ten years old. Too young to understand the politics, but old enough to feel the hatred directed toward my family everywhere we went." He slowed down at the guard's gate.

"Guten abend," Gustav said, with a stiff salute.

Will waved and entered the gate, continuing to Amy, "It wasn't until I was older that I learned what had happened. By then, I had been given the crown and had no one to turn it over to in order to make things right. Until I found you, that is."

He drew to a halt outside the palace but didn't make a move to get out.

"Didn't you like being a prince at all?" Amy asked, wondering how someone's conscience could be so strong that it could even take away the fun of being royalty.

"Of course I did," he admitted, and she was glad to hear him say it. "I'm human. There are some very nice perks to this position." He looked at her, his face only partially illuminated by the outdoor lights. "But it's very difficult for a man to truly feel good about his place when he knows he's come to it by unjust means."

Amy's heart constricted. He was so beautiful, and so earnest, that part of her wanted to reach over and kiss him right now. "Is that why you haven't married? So that you don't continue a line you feel is illegitimate?"

His eyes locked on hers. "You are perceptive."

"Not really. I'm just curious. It's interesting to try to understand where people are coming from." It was particularly interesting to try to understand Will, but she didn't add that.

"What about you? Why haven't you stayed in a relationship for long?"

"Haven't found the right man."

"Ah." He nodded. "That's an easy answer."

"It's the truth."

"All right. But what would make someone the right man?"

She smiled. "Hard to say. He'd have to be honest. I mean *really* honest. That's number one. And he'd have to have integrity. No losers trying to get a free ride in life. Ambition would be good and a sense of humor is a must. And I don't care what he looks like as long as he makes my pulse race when I see him." As soon as she'd spoken, she realized she'd described Will. She looked down, hoping he wouldn't see it in her face. "That's all. I'm not all that demanding." She met his eyes. "What would you look for in a woman? If you dared to have a relationship, I mean."

He didn't smile but kept his eyes on her steadily. "Inner beauty. That light in her eyes that comes from a happy and peaceful soul." He reached over and touched her cheek. "Like that light in your eyes."

She caught her breath.

"I also treasure honesty," he went on, his voice low. "And intelligence. And the kind of integrity that would prevent her from taking a bag of gold if she thought she wasn't entitled to it."

Silence lingered between them as he gently caressed her cheek with his knuckles.

"So what's stopping you?" she asked breathlessly. "I mean, from finding that woman and being with her?"

He drew his hand back. "Many things. Not the least of which is the fact that I might not be the appropriate choice for someone like that."

She wanted the moment back, but it was slipping away like a waning tide. "Why wouldn't you let *her* make that choice?"

"Because I have to do what I know is right." He nodded, more to himself than to her, then said, "No matter how difficult that might be." He took the keys out of the ignition and got out of the car.

This time Amy didn't wait for him to open the door for her. She got out herself and they walked in silence toward the palace steps.

He opened the door for her and helped her out of

her coat, but didn't say anything more than a few polite words about having enjoyed the evening with her and hoping she slept well.

She returned the courtesy, and by the time they parted ways, they felt like two complete strangers.

She went to her room alone, feeling far emptier than a girl who had just been offered the role of princess had any right to, and she lay in the dark until finally, close to dawn, she fell asleep.

Will could not sleep. He kept replaying his conversation with Amé in his head. She'd asked what his ideal woman was, and he'd described her. He hadn't meant to, it had just come out that way. The more he'd said, the more he'd realized that the woman he was describing as the one person he could share his life with was the one person he could absolutely *not* get too close to.

If he wanted a woman, there was a fairly large field of choices out there for him. Yet ever since he'd gotten back from the United States with Amé, she was the only woman on his mind. It didn't matter what he was thinking about, his thoughts kept trailing back to her. He kept recalling the softness of her lips under his, the satin touch of her skin and the feeling of running his fingers through her hair. It wasn't enough. The memories of a few scant kisses were wearing thin. He wanted more.

This was dangerous.

And he knew exactly what he had to do.

When he was younger, Will had spent several years

in the Lufthanian military. One thing he'd learned, not just from his own experiences but from those of the men around him, was that it was nearly impossible to be effective in executing a task if you were distracted by something you perceived as better or more interesting. This was why they tended to take the men into the mountains for boot camp and training—they had to get them away from their women and families, and all the comforts of home.

So it made sense that Will should take a page from that book and remove himself from his own object of distraction. He had to distance himself from Amé so he could regain his sense of purpose.

It was the only way he could do what he knew was right.

Chapter Seven

The next afternoon, after hearing nothing from Will all morning, Amy was surprised when he came to her as she was leaving lunch.

"I understand you've been inquiring about airline flights back to the United States," he said, without preamble.

"Yes, I have. I have to be realistic about what might happen next. You might get those test results and kick me right out of the palace."

"You know that isn't so."

"I don't *know* anything."

He looked at her in silence for a moment, then took her arm. "Come with me."

"Wait—where?" she asked, being dragged helplessly along with him.

"I want to show you something."

"What?"

"You'll see."

He led her to a wide hallway she had not yet seen, and stopped in front of one of at least twenty-five oil portraits.

"You see this?" he asked, gesturing toward the painting of an old man with a long gray beard that made him look exactly like Father Time. "That is your great-great grandfather, King Leopold II. He was a hero during the Great War, and is still remembered for his humanitarian policies."

"I—"

"And this…" Will said, his voice terse. He indicated another painting, this one of a young woman with glossy dark hair piled high on her head and delicate ringlets framing her blue-eyed beauty. She held a baby in her arms, and had the sweetest expression of serenity. "This is your great-grandmother. She died during World War I while smuggling refugees out of France, when the train they were on was bombed. She left behind a toddler, your grandfather." He pointed at the baby.

Amy's breath caught in her chest. It was hard to imagine that kind of courage and heroism, but it was the baby who touched her most. A child left alone in such tumultuous times. It broke her heart.

Will led her farther down the hall. "This," he said, pointing at a painting of a young boy with a white pony, "is your uncle Frederick. Or it would have been. He died a year after this portrait was painted, when he lost his life to childhood leukemia."

Amy swallowed hard, looking at the sweet-faced boy who had died so young. She couldn't even imagine the toll it must have taken on his parents.

Will didn't wait for a response. He pulled her farther down the hall and stopped in front of a portrait of a middle-aged couple. The portrait was different, in that the paint was scarred in places and the frame looked new. "These are your grandparents," he said solemnly. "Look at your grandmother's face. Look at her eyes." He pointed, then looked at Amy. "Are those not the eyes you look at in the mirror every morning when you wash your face, and every evening when you brush your teeth?"

"I don't know!" She was on the verge of losing her composure. "I'm so afraid."

"Afraid? What on earth do you have to fear? Is the prospect of your Lufthanian heritage so terrible?"

"No, that's not it at all." She swallowed a lump in her throat. "What's terrifying is to come all this way, to begin to believe and to feel at home here, only to find out it's all been a mistake. Where would I be then?" She couldn't even bear to think of coming so close to finding her real parents, even if only in the memory of others, only to have it slip through her fingers.

"Amé." Will took her by the shoulders, his grip hard against her skin. "There is no mistake. I don't understand why you're so reluctant to accept this."

"Because I'm not the type of person that this kind of thing happens to," she said. "It's not that I'm jinxed or anything, but my life tends to have a lot of close calls without ever really...I don't know...I'm just not particularly lucky.''

Will looked at her steadily before saying, ''Your luck is about to change.''

''You don't know how much I hope you're right,'' she said quietly.

''Come with me.'' He led her into the nearest room and took her to the window. A broad sweep of snowy valley lay before them, dotted with barns and little farmhouses with smoke rising from their chimneys. ''This is your land. Your country. This is where you were born. This is where your family worked the soil, fought for their freedoms, died for their country.'' His eyes softened. ''Amé, this...'' He let go of her and gestured at their surroundings. ''Right here, where we stand, this building is where you were born. Your first breath still lingers in the air here.''

Her eyes burned, and her throat felt as if it had swelled shut.

''You know this is the truth,'' Will went on. ''I can see it in your eyes. I saw it the moment you laid eyes on the castle.''

It was true, as soon as she'd seen the castle of Lufthania, it was as if someone had struck a haunting minor chord of familiarity. But she had attributed that to the fact that the castle looked like the fairy tale abode she'd imagined in every story her mother had read to her as a child. She'd imagined it a thousand times or more, with its snow-peaked spires and shadowy eaves.

And here was Will, looking every inch the part of the handsome prince.

"Last night when I was trying to go to sleep," she said, "you know that feeling when you're halfway between being asleep and awake?"

He nodded.

"Well, I kept hearing snippets of conversations. Voices I couldn't identify, yet I felt like I knew them. I don't know if it was a dream, or my imagination or actual memories, but for the first time I really believed that maybe you were right about who I am." She shrugged, so full of emotion she thought she might burst. "If it's all a mistake, I don't know what I'll do."

"You have absolutely nothing to worry about," Will told her tenderly. "I promise you that. You will truly live happily ever after."

"Excuse me, sir." An elderly gentleman entered, holding a newspaper. "I'm sorry to interrupt but I've been looking for you."

Will turned and looked surprised. "Yes, Franz?"

"Franz?" Amy repeated, sniffing and trying to regain her composure.

Will cleared his throat. "Yes, Amelia, this is Franz Burgess. My private secretary."

"Franz Burgess." She gave Will a look, glad for a little levity, and held her hand out to the older man. "I've heard so much about you. I'm glad to *finally* meet you."

Franz looked at her extended hand for a moment, then took it awkwardly and gave a bow. "Thank you,

Miss Scott.'' He turned his attention back to Will. ''If I may have a private word with you, sir…?''

Will looked put out. ''Is privacy absolutely necessary?''

''Perhaps you can decide for yourself.'' He handed the newspaper to Will.

He opened it and even from a couple of feet away, Amy couldn't help but notice the large picture of herself on the front page. ''Hey, what's that?'' She reached for the paper and read the headline.

De Verlorene Prinzessin von Lufthania ist zurückge kommen.

Not for the first time since she'd arrived, she wished she'd taken German in high school instead of French.

''What does it say?''

Will's face was still with concentration as he read. ''That the lost princess of Lufthania has returned. That a palace insider has confirmed this.'' He folded the paper and handed it back to Franz. ''Who is responsible for this?''

''I do not know, sir.''

''Any ideas?''

''No, sir.'' Franz's face betrayed nothing. Amy guessed he would make a great poker player.

Will sighed. ''Was it not made clear to the staff that Amelia's presence here was to remain confidential until the test results were final?''

''It was made clear,'' Franz confirmed. ''But the media can be very determined. Sometimes it isn't possible to hide the truth from them.''

Amy watched this exchange curiously. Was Will

accusing Franz of leaking the news? Was Franz setting up his own defense by saying the media could get what they wanted no matter what?

It didn't occur to her that it could have any implications for her until Will dismissed Franz and turned to her with an apology. "I don't know who would have done this. I assure you that this kind of breach of privacy doesn't usually occur here."

She shrugged. "Does it really matter that much? Surely you can call the paper and have them set the story straight for tomorrow's edition."

He shook his head. "You don't understand. For twenty-five years a good number of people in this country have been hungry for your family's return to the throne. Now that the story is out, I'm afraid it won't be easy to hide. Particularly since it's the truth."

She sighed. She wasn't going to argue about that again. "Surely you were prepared for the possibility the press would find out I was here. I still don't see why this is such a huge deal."

"Because now you are expected. Now your people want to see you, to hear from you. They want to know that you're staying."

"But I'm probably not!"

He splayed his arms. "Then you see the problem."

She did. "Do you think the reporter who wrote this might take some kind of quote from you, or even from me, about how this is a mistake?"

"I'm not going to say that this is a mistake." He walked to the window. "I've made plenty of mistakes in my life, and I'll take full credit for all of them, but not this. *This* is no mistake.''

Already she knew him well enough to believe him. He wasn't about to make a public announcement that she was *not* Princess Amelia.

She could even see the problem with doing that before the test results proved or disproved it conclusively. There was a possibility—even she was prepared to admit it—that the results would be positive.

In that case... Well, in that case she didn't know *what* she would do. She couldn't even allow herself to think about it yet. She wanted—no, she *needed*—to be prepared for the worst. And the worst would be if she found out, after all of this, that she didn't belong. That she was still, underneath it all, an anonymous orphan.

''When will the test results come back?'' she asked.

He shrugged. ''I've asked them to rush. It may be within the week.''

She calculated when the winter ball was, since that was the first royal event in which her identity would be questioned publicly. It was six days away. People could speculate all they wanted within that time. ''Then we'll just have to wait it out,'' she said.

He looked at her for a moment, then laughed.

''What's so funny?''

''You still don't understand your importance here, do you?''

''So far, I have no importance here,'' she said defiantly.

''At this point,'' he said, too patiently, ''it ceases

to matter *what* the test results say. At least as far as the Lufthanian people are concerned. Your picture has appeared on the front page of the newspaper, looking, incidentally, so like your mother that it's unmistakable. A palace *insider* has confirmed that you are, indeed, the missing Princess Amelia.'' He expelled a long breath. ''This will not go away.''

''Meaning…?'' She had the ominous feeling that whatever he was getting at required more of her than of anyone else.

''Meaning you are expected to be the princess. Now.''

''But I can't!'' The whole idea was so absurd, she could barely formulate a response. ''I can't just *be* a princess because the newspapers want one.'' She threw her hands up in the air. ''Can't you just tell the press about the pending blood test?''

''And cast your legitimacy into doubt?'' He scoffed. ''When you are formally welcomed back—and you will be—it must be without any shadow of doubt having ever been placed on you.''

''Okay, I can see that. But why say anything at all, then? Why would I need to make a public appearance before, say, the winter ball next week? I can just be the quiet, mysterious visitor.''

Will turned around and snapped his fingers. ''That's it! You're a genius.''

''No, I'm not—''

He shot her a silencing look, but it was tinged with humor. ''I'll have Franz announce that you're not making your first public appearance until the ball. By then you, and anyone else who wants it, will have definitive proof.'' He nodded, pleased with himself. ''That will work.''

She didn't answer right away. If the blood test results came back positive, and if she truly *was* the missing Princess Amelia, then she *would* have a duty to the country.

Wouldn't she?

She wasn't entirely sure how to think about that, or how to decide just *what* that duty would be, or how far she needed to go to fulfill it. But certainly she couldn't just turn her back on Lufthania.

Or on Will.

He had come so far to find her. Done so much. And he'd done it all with the best interests of his people at heart. The act of abdicating the throne was so completely selfless, she felt terrible even contemplating leaving him to this position he didn't want.

She wasn't sure she wanted the position, either. Sure, it was glamorous to sit in Dentytown and imagine being a princess, but now that she was here she saw the tremendous responsibility that went along with the job.

Then again, if it was true and she was Princess Amelia, she was the *only* possible heir. She couldn't refuse the position in favor of a younger sibling, or a cousin, or anyone else. If she was Princess Amelia, it was up to her or Will. That was it.

And if she refused the position, and it *had* to be

Will, he would have to abandon his hopes of actually helping his country in a substantial way.

The weight of her predicament settled heavily on her shoulders. For the first time, she understood the serious implications that Will had been wrestling with all this time.

"Let's just say you're right," she said slowly. "What then?"

He looked surprised. "If I'm right about what? About you?"

She couldn't even say the words. She merely nodded.

He smiled. "So you are starting to see it."

"No," she objected quickly. "No, I'm just asking you *theoretically*. What would happen if I—or anyone—turned out to be the missing princess?"

To his credit, he didn't leap on her question with a triumphant *Aha!* Instead, he answered her matter-of-factly. "The transition would be smooth, except for a great deal of celebration in the country. And, to be honest, probably a bit of media coverage."

"But what, exactly, would happen? Would you just stand in the town square and announce there's a new monarch or what?"

He smiled. "It would be announced from the palace. As would my abdication. You would be introduced formally as the princess and take up residence here. You would be given a private secretary, who would arrange your appearances and charitable engagements. Then,'' he said, shrugging, ''you could do whatever you like.''

She nodded thoughtfully. ''Anything?''

''Your life is your own.''

''So, then my family truly could come and stay? Indefinitely? Or my friends?''

''Of course,'' he answered. ''There is no strict protocol for you to follow. You could write your own script, so to speak.''

For one crazy moment, she could imagine it. She could see herself living in Lufthania and waking up daily to this beautiful landscape.

Thing was, when she pictured it, she pictured Will. For some reason, he was all wrapped up in her picture of Lufthania and of palace life. It was more difficult for her to picture herself alone in the palace than here with him.

''Are you considering staying, or trying to think of a way to tell me you're leaving?'' Will asked, bringing Amy out of her thoughts.

She hesitated. ''I'm wishing the test results would come back so I would know whether or not there was really anything for me to consider.''

He touched her cheek. ''There is much for you to consider,'' he said, looking deeply into her eyes. ''Make no mistake about that.''

She swallowed but said nothing.

Their gazes lingered on each other for a moment.

Then, suddenly, Will was brisk. ''I have business to attend to,'' he said, stepping away from her. ''I trust you can make it back to your rooms.''

She nodded. "No problem. I'll find my way."

"Good. I'll see you later, then. I hope you'll think about what I said."

He barely waited for her response before turning and striding from the room.

Amy stood still, listening to his footsteps recede down the hall and disappear before she let out a long, pent-up breath.

But she wouldn't breathe fully until the test results came back.

Will strode from the room and straight down to his office, although he couldn't imagine getting any work done right now. Amé was an incredible distraction. He could well imagine spending the next twelve months anticipating her appearance in the mornings and tossing repartee back and forth with her all day.

What he imagined for the nights didn't bear thinking about.

He knew from the outset that this was an emotional situation for him. How could it not be? Despite his feeling of illegitimacy, he had been groomed nearly his entire life for the position he was trying so desperately to abandon now. And there was no guarantee he could succeed in the civil service. He was going to have to begin small and run for public office at the next election. It was entirely possible that the people wouldn't elect him.

But then again, if they didn't want to elect him to office, then surely they didn't want him as their prince, either.

By that logic, there was no way he was doing the wrong thing. Being right didn't make it any easier to do.

If Amé had been homely, it would have been easier. Homely and dull. And eager to take the throne. That would have been perfect. He could have passed the reins to her and moved on without looking back.

But when he contemplated leaving Amé, it was much more difficult. It wasn't that he thought she couldn't handle the position. He knew she could. She was a strong, vibrant woman, with more than enough energy for everything she'd have to do. She didn't need him.

It was worse. He was starting to fear that he, given half a chance, might end up needing her. And that prospect was intolerable.

When he got to his office, he found Franz there, talking on the telephone. When his eyes alighted on Will, he held up a hand, thanked whomever he was speaking with and promised to call them back, then hung up the receiver.

"What are you still doing here, Franz?" Will asked, checking his watch. "Shouldn't you have gone half an hour ago?"

"I'm afraid something has come up," Franz said, jotting something on a notepad. "A small matter of state."

"What is it?"

"A cousin to the Princess of Carsoria has passed away. The Duchess of Kalone. We'll need to send a representative to the funeral."

"When is it?"

"The day after tomorrow. I was thinking perhaps General Heim—"

"I'll go."

Franz looked surprised. "I beg your pardon?"

"I said I'll go to the funeral. I met the duchess several times and liked her very much. A lovely young woman."

"She was ninety-four. Perhaps you have her confused with someone else."

Will tried to hide his irritation. He wanted to get away for a few days, to collect himself and hopefully shake this disturbing interest he was developing in Amé. This was the perfect excuse. "This may be my last royal duty, Franz. I'll do it."

"Very well, sir." Franz nodded uncertainly. "I'll make the arrangements."

"Good." Will went to look out the window so Franz couldn't read anything into his expression. "I'll leave first thing tomorrow morning." He turned to face Franz. "I trust you will help Amé if she needs anything?"

"As you wish."

Will nodded, satisfied. "Excellent. Then I'll go tomorrow and come back in a few days. By then maybe the DNA test results will be complete and we can make a formal announcement of Amé's return."

Chapter Eight

"He's gone?" Amy tried to fight the panic that rose in her breast.

"Only for a few days, dear." Letty patted her shoulder. "I know you'll miss him, but absence does make the heart grow fonder."

"It's not that I miss him," Amy objected. "It's just that, who knows what kind of disaster I'll make of things?"

Letty looked thoughtful. "You need Prince Wilhelm here to protect you."

"Exactly." Amy flopped down on the wing chair in her room. "God help me. "My foremothers are spinning in their graves."

Letty clicked her tongue against her teeth. "Nonsense, child. There are times when only one person fully understands the role you are expected to fulfill,

and he is not here. It isn't weak for you to be afraid.
It is normal.''

Amy's eyes filled with burning gratitude. ''Thank
you.'' But she was still uncomfortable with Will's absence. She understood why a funeral would cause him
to leave unexpectedly, but so quickly that he couldn't
even say goodbye? Not that she felt he owed her an
explanation or anything, but she had kind of felt they
were getting closer. Forget the kiss—he had been so
sensitive to her, so caring. It just didn't seem like him
to up and leave without a word like that.

Then again, she didn't *really* know him.

''Let's prepare you for the week ahead, shall we?''
Letty said with confidence.

''Thanks, Letty. I don't know what I'd do if you
weren't here.''

''It wasn't easy to get along without you, either, my
child. I'm so very glad you're back. If only your mama
were here…'' Letty's voice trailed off and for a moment she appeared lost in time. Then she snapped back
and said, ''We must find your dress for the ball.'' She
went to the closet and threw open the door. ''Did you
bring something formal?''

''Yes,'' Amy began. ''It's in the closet.''

''Where?'' Letty asked, moving the hangers full of
clothes aside one by one. ''Is it in here?'' She took
the formal gown Amy had bought from Burdell's last
month and moved it aside along with the rest. ''I don't
see it.''

Amy's face grew warm as she reached in and pulled
out the dress Letty had just moved aside. ''Here it is.''

Letty looked at the simple black dress, then at Amy. "This? Oh, no, no, no, my dear. This will never do."

"Why not? Isn't it fancy enough?"

"That is a cocktail dress," Letty explained. "What you need is a formal ball gown. Let me see what I can do." She lifted the telephone receiver and punched in three numbers, then spoke in German to someone on the other end of the line. When she hung up, she turned to Amy and said, "Fear not. You will have a dress by tomorrow."

"From where?"

"I'm having Lufthania's finest designer, Eldine, bring some dresses over for you."

"That's really not necessary—"

Letty would hear none of that. "I wonder if you'd also like something done to your hair." She flipped her fingers through Amy's long, straight hair.

Amy had to laugh. She wasn't insulted by Letty's suggestion. Her friends had told her more than once that it looked more like 1970s Cher than was flattering. "You know, Letty," she said, "I'm up for anything. In fact, I'd welcome a change."

"How exciting!" Letty exclaimed. "Then I shall have the hairdresser, a manicurist and an aesthetician come in. Oh, and I'll have Eldine bring several designs for you, not just ball gowns."

"Are you sure Prince Wilhelm won't mind?" Amy asked.

"Darling," Letty said, beaming at Amy. "He will be delighted. Trust me."

Two days later, Amy's hair was about six inches shorter, cut into flattering layers that framed her face. Her skin was smooth and glowing from the facial Letty had arranged, and she had a closet full of expensive designer clothes that fit her as if they had been sewn for her alone. What's more, Eldine refused to accept any payment for them, which Amy thought was incredibly generous. Letty said later that Eldine knew that the exposure she would get with Amy wearing her clothes was far better than any advertising she could pay for, but Amy was still touched by the gesture.

She was feeling much more confident that evening as she sat in the window seat of her room, watching the snow drift slowly down and sipping Letty's wonderful hot chocolate.

She was waiting for Letty to bring her a refill when there was a knock on her door.

"Come on in, Letty, you don't need to knock." She turned on the window seat just as the door opened and Will came in.

His glossy dark hair was mussed, as if it had been a long day and he hadn't bothered to look in a mirror. He was still wearing a dark wool overcoat, which was dotted with snow, and there was a weariness in his eyes that she hadn't seen before.

"Letty is giving us some time alone," he said. "You can ring for her later."

"Is everything all right?" Amy asked.

"Your DNA test results have come back." He produced a torn envelope from his pocket.

Suddenly she didn't want to know. She hadn't begun to think of herself as royalty, but the faces in the paintings Will had shown her had become her friends. In the two days he'd been gone, she must have returned to the portrait hall at least a half a dozen times, studying the faces and wondering if it was truly possible that they were her family.

They had begun to *feel* like kin, though it was possible that she felt that way out of the sheer power of wanting to belong. The imagination was a powerful thing, especially when combined with her heart's desire to know where she came from.

"May I sit down?" Will asked, indicating the chair opposite her.

"Of course," she said, pulling her robe closer to her.

"Are you cold?" He took his coat off and held it out to her.

"No, I'm not cold. I'm just a little…" Scared? Hopeful? Both? She didn't bother to try to articulate her feelings. "Are those the results there?" She pointed to the envelope.

"They are." It was obvious the envelope had been opened in haste. He handed it to her but said, "The details are in German but the conclusion is clear."

"And…?" She swallowed hard.

He looked at her, as if seeing her for the first time. His gaze, though weary, was penetrating. "And you are the Princess Amelia."

Her breath left her in one long, shuddering stream.

"Are you sure?" she asked, barely daring to hope. "Is there any chance there could be a mistake?"

"The test result accuracy exceeds 99.99 percent," he said. "They tested sixteen markers, then ran all exclusions twice for confirmation. There is no mistake."

She didn't fully understand the science of it. She'd been more interested in English in school. But his conclusion, and the conclusion of the lab, was clear. "Do you promise me," she said, her voice weak with emotion, "that you haven't fudged the results in order to get the princess you need so desperately?"

He laughed so spontaneously that she had to believe it was sincere. "Amé, if I were so desperate for a princess that I would go to those measures, I assure you I could have found a much more willing and predictable candidate than you."

She had to smile. "I guess you're right."

"I promise you," he said, looking deeply into her eyes. "I would not lie to you."

Her breath caught in her throat, but she tried to keep things light. "Is that right? Franz?"

His face colored slightly. "You have my word that I will never attempt to deceive you again."

She believed him. "So what happens now?"

"That is up to you. I want you to stay. But you are not a captive here. You must listen to your heart and decide from that."

She gave a laugh. "My heart has been unreliable lately."

"Oh?" He looked interested. "In what way?"

She felt her face grow warm. "That doesn't matter. The real issue here is whether I stay in Lufthania and honor my biological family or if I should go back to the United States where my *real* family is."

"Must the two be mutually exclusive? I've told you that you can send for your family and have them live here with you."

She tried to imagine how her parents would react to that, but she couldn't. There was a possibility they would be willing. But if they weren't, and she had to move three thousand miles away from them, that would be a difficult decision to make.

"They already live some distance from you, don't they?" he asked, as if reading her mind.

"They do," she conceded. They'd only moved to Florida three months ago, but they seemed to enjoy it, so there was little hope that they'd move back to Maryland. And there was no way on earth Amy was going to move to a tropical climate, no matter how much she loved her parents.

So that wasn't really a consideration.

"What is it, Amé?" he asked, taking her hands in his. "Why do you hesitate?"

She thought about it for a moment before answering. "Because the princess aspect of this is still unbelievable to me," she said. Her eyes suddenly burned with tears. "I can't tell you how much it means to me to find out who my parents were. It was so painful all of those years, knowing that they had died anonymously and believing that there was no one in the

world who cared about their—well, *our*—fate." She
brushed tears off her cheeks.

"Can you remember them at all?"

She shook her head. "I don't think so. Now and
then I have these moments when I have what feels like
a memory, but I can't quite grasp it. A scent might
trigger it. Or a few notes of music. It might sound
crazy, but even a particular kind of day, when it's
dreary and gray and the trees are like skeletons against
the sky, *almost* reminds me of something, but as soon
as I try to think about it, it's gone. And I feel lost all
over again."

"You aren't lost anymore, Amé." There was sor-
row in his eyes, but warmth and tenderness, too. "You
are found." He cupped his hand on her cheek. "Finally."

She put her hand on his. "It's hard to really believe." She swallowed. "I mean, it's hard to accept,
you know? I've spent a lifetime with this uncertainty.
It's hard to believe all those huge questions are finally
answered. I keep waiting for the other shoe to fall."

"There is no other shoe." He went to her and knelt
before her, taking her hands in his. "Unless it is a
glass slipper."

She rolled her eyes. "For that, you need a handsome
prince."

He drew back.

It took her a moment to realize what she'd said.
"Oh! Will, I didn't mean you weren't—"

"I'm not," he said seriously, releasing her hands
and standing up. "I'm no Prince Charming."

"Yes you are," she insisted. "That's exactly what you are. All *I* meant was that…I…well, I haven't had the best of luck with men."

Will sat down on the chair. "What was his name? Ben something?"

"Singer," she supplied, leaning back heavily. She didn't want to think about Ben right now. "And he doesn't matter anymore."

"If you say so."

She hated to give Ben credit for anything at this point, including her mistrust in relationships, though he probably had some role to play in that. But the more obvious problem for her was that of losing her parents at three and never seeing them again, apparently not even understanding the explanations given to her in English right after the accident. It wasn't hard to see how a person might develop a fear of abandonment after something like that.

The frustrating thing was that recognizing it didn't seem to take her very far on the path to overcoming it.

Rather than dissect her psyche, though, she decided to turn the tables on Will. "What about *you?*" she asked.

"What about me?"

"You're awfully quick to question me on my romantic history, but you don't say much about your own."

He shrugged. "There isn't much to say." His face was so handsome by the low light of her bedroom that

she couldn't even *imagine* that there wasn't a lot
to say.

And she wanted to hear every word of it.

"Somehow I find it hard to believe," she said, "that
Prince Wilhelm, idol of women all over Europe, thinks
there isn't much to say about his romantic life. I'll bet
if I looked in the newspaper archives, I'd find plenty."

"You wouldn't find anything pleasant," he said, his
voice grim. He stood up. "It's time for me to go."

"Wait." She immediately felt bad for touching a
nerve. She stood and went to him. "I'm sorry. I
shouldn't have teased you."

He touched her hand and hesitated for a moment
before saying, "I was engaged several years back. My
fiancée was killed in an accident. That is what you'd
find in the newspaper archives."

"I'm so sorry." She'd been known to put her foot
in her mouth before, but this was the worst. She put
her hand on his forearm. "Honestly, I had no idea."

He looked at her hand, then shifted his gaze to her
eyes. A long moment passed, with only heartbeats between them.

"I know," he said at last, disengaging himself from
her touch. "Tomorrow morning we will discuss the
formal announcement to be made at the winter ball.
Please make a decision as to what you intend to do."

She nodded, still feeling just awful about opening
that wound for him. "I will."

He gave a curt nod. "I'll send Franz for you around
ten."

"Sure." She stood awkwardly, wishing he wouldn't

go yet. She wanted to say something—*anything*—to smooth things over with him and just make it feel like it did before. But no words came to her.

He turned to leave.

"Will, please…"

He stopped and turned back. "Yes?" His voice was impersonal, as if every inch of physical distance between them added a degree of chill to their relationship.

"Was she…were you…" She was going to say close, but what a foolish question that would be. Of course they were close, they were engaged. Frantically, she searched for something else to say. "I just wanted to say I'm really, really sorry."

He gave a tight smile. "I'll see you in the morning, Amé."

"See you." She gave a small wave.

He left and she stood, holding her breath for a moment before flopping down on the bed. What an incredibly awkward situation that had been. She'd marched headlong into it but found herself completely unable to retreat. She hated that she'd put him on the spot that way.

How could she hold a highly visible public position when she wasn't even capable of smoothing over an uncomfortable moment in a private conversation?

She went to the window and looked out at the moonlit valley, the snow glowing like phosphorescence through the dark. It was so beautiful it made her ache.

And maybe…just maybe…it *was* familiar. Something about the curve of the hill to the west, and the way the trees were sprinkled like chocolate jimmies over the white-ice-cream mountains brought her a deep sense of peace and happiness. She'd been here before, back before she knew what sadness and loneliness were. Before she knew what it was like to lose someone, or to be afraid.

This was home.

Suddenly she knew it. *This* was home. She'd looked out this very window twenty-five years before, her mother's warm breath on her neck, pointing a slender finger to the hills and saying... Amy concentrated. What had her mother said to her? Words she didn't understand floated around in her head. *Mein herz...*

Mein herz ist immer hier mit Ihnen.

It rang, as clear as a bell, in her mind.

But what did it mean?

She made a mental note to ask someone tomorrow and returned her thoughts to the situation at hand.

She was Princess Amelia Louisa Gretchen May. It didn't matter that she didn't *feel* as if she was, the medical evidence had proved it.

And the facts bore it out. Had it not been for the princess element, she could have believed Will's story much sooner. The puzzle pieces fit together—a couple, leaving their war-torn country with a baby in tow, trying to keep their anonymity so that no one knew who they were. There could not be worse circumstances under which to have a fatal accident, but they had, and it had resulted in the very strange predicament of a princess being raised in a small-town American family, with no idea of who she was or where she came from.

It was hard to believe, but truth *was,* as they said, stranger than fiction.

Amy's truth was just stranger than any fiction she'd ever read.

But none of that mattered. She knew where she came from now, and she knew what she had to do about it. Her family had loved her, she was certain of it. And they had loved this country. It was her moral duty to carry on as they would have, if they could have. It was her duty to take the throne back, in honor of her mother and her father and her grandparents, and in honor of everyone who had loved them and sworn allegiance to them.

Not that she thought she could offer what her family before her could have. She couldn't. But maybe, just by the fact of her *being,* the fact of her surviving, she could give some people hope.

Plus she could help Will do what he felt the country needed. Amy trusted Will. She trusted his opinion and judgment. If he thought he could make a positive change for the people of Lufthania, but only if Amy took over his position as monarch, she would do it.

After all, it didn't mean abandoning her old life. She could bring her parents here. Her friends. Heck, she could even continue to conduct her business from the computer if she wanted to.

A cold, hard look at her life told her that there really wasn't that much to miss if she moved. And it wasn't as if she was moving to another planet, anyway. If she wanted to go back to Maryland she could do so at any time. Maybe not to live, not once the announcement was made that she was Princess Amelia, but she could visit as often as she wanted. If she wanted.

Although she'd enjoyed her business tremendously, it wasn't as if it had made her feel truly worthwhile in the grand scheme of things. Being self-sufficient was a good feeling, but it didn't make a difference in other peoples' lives. Now she had that opportunity.

She was going to take it. And she was going to take it with gusto. She would give it her all, as she had never done before. If she didn't succeed, in the end no one would be able to accuse her of not trying her best.

Life had given her a brilliant opportunity and she'd hung back like a whiny child, afraid to touch it for fear it would disappear.

Well, it wasn't disappearing.

And neither was she.

Chapter Nine

Will barely got a wink of sleep.

When had he become so clumsy in conversation? He'd tripped so badly over the subject of his romantic involvements when he was talking to Amé that it was a wonder he hadn't ended up with bruises.

Worse, he knew he'd left her with the feeling that she'd been the one to take the misstep.

The truth was that Amé had come so close to capturing his heart that he'd panicked. If he'd stayed in that room with her one more moment, he wouldn't have been able to stop himself from carrying her to the bed and making love to her, and he knew—he knew without any doubt—that nothing could be worse for the two of them.

He couldn't be her lover. For heaven's sake, he was her *enemy*. His family had killed hers and usurped

their place. It was the fault of his family and their
regime that Princess Lily had been forced to leave her
home and try to forge her way, with her family, in a
strange country. If not for the coup, Lily would reign
right now and Amé would never have suffered the
trauma of losing her parents. To say nothing of her
country and her birthright.

If he couldn't live with that, how on earth could he
expect her to?

Granted, she was uncertain right now. She wasn't
sure what her place was or how to assert it. It was his
duty to help her with that. But once she gained the
confidence he knew she would, she would recognize
that he had no place in her life.

"Sir." Franz's voice brought Will back to the present, which was shortly before 10:00 a.m. in his office.
"Would you like for me to go for Her Highness
now?"

It was on the tip of Will's tongue to volunteer to
do it himself, but instead he gave a short nod. He
didn't need to go to Amy's bedroom again. He would
keep things impersonal. His office was the perfect
place for that. "Thank you, Franz."

Franz wasn't gone five minutes before he gave a
cursory knock on Will's door and opened it, announcing, "Her Highness, Princess Amelia."

Amé entered, giving a disbelieving look at Franz as
she passed him. When he closed the door behind her,
she looked at Will and said, "*That* is going to take
some getting used to."

"I doubt it will take long. After all, you have been here before."

"Yes, for nearly ten percent of my life." She smiled. "Unfortunately, since it was the first ten percent, it isn't helping me much now."

"Then I shall help you instead," he said. "Please, take a seat." He gestured at the chair in front of his desk.

She sat.

"Here is the plan. The winter ball is in four days. In that time, Franz will tell the media that an official announcement will be made from the palace on that evening."

"Doesn't everyone already know what that announcement will be?"

"It doesn't matter. They can speculate about it in advance. The announcement is a formality. But it's a vital formality. Until that time, you are not officially the princess royal."

"Don't you need to step down as crown prince in order for that to happen?" she asked. She was holding steady onto her composure, but he could tell she was nervous.

"I'll do so in my introduction," he said. "We needn't make an enormous issue of it. The legalities will be taken care of behind the scenes."

She swallowed. "If you say so." She shifted in her seat. "Will I be expected to make some kind of speech at that point? Please say no."

"No." He couldn't help but smile. "You will give

a press conference later, of course, but you will be well coached in advance."

"By whom?"

"Franz or myself." He shrugged. "There are plenty of people who will be available to help you with your official duties."

"Easy for you to say." She took a long breath. "You're not the one they're going to talk about if you use the wrong fork for your salad."

"Letty can explain the basics of etiquette to you, if necessary."

"Actually, I had a home ec teacher in high school who was Princess Di's number one fan, so I don't think that's going to be a problem, but you're missing my point. I just want to know what to expect and what's expected of me *before* I'm faced with it."

"Understandable. I'll take you through it step by step."

"Thank you." She looked relieved. "Okay, so you make the announcement, then I…what? What do I do then?"

"Smile and wave."

She thought about it. "Well, I'm telling you right now, I'm not learning to do any goofy royalty wave." She held up a cupped hand, fingers tightly together, and turned it side to side. "That thing. I'm not doing it."

He laughed. She was irresistible. Every time he thought he could cut their ties and send her on her way, she did something else that endeared her to him.

"But that is a grand tradition among European royalty."

"I don't care, I'm not doing it." She shook her head. "It stops here."

"Very well, then, when the announcement is made, you may curtsey—"

"You're joking, right?"

He kept a straight face. "I'm sorry?"

"You want me to curtsey? On some kind of podium in front of everyone? Uh-uh. No way." She eyed him suspiciously. "You are joking, right?"

"Right again."

She smiled. "Some help you turned out to be. So what happens next?"

"Next you, as the hostess of the evening, open the dancing with the first dance."

"Very funny."

"No, no, I'm serious."

She looked at him in disbelief for a moment, then, seeing the look on his face, changed her expression to one of panic. "I have to dance the first dance?"

He nodded. "With a partner, of course. You won't be expected to stand before the crowd and pirouette and so on." If this was the biggest of her worries, she would have an easy time of it. "What is the problem?"

"I can't dance."

"Not a simple waltz?"

She shook her head.

"One, two, three." He moved his fingers on the desk in illustration.

"Nope. Surely we can bypass that part."

"It is tradition."

She shrugged. "Things are about to change, anyway."

He braced his hands on his desk for a moment, thinking. "Not this." He lifted the telephone receiver. "I'll simply get you a dance instructor. It won't take long."

She sighed. "Okay. I guess it's something I'll have to learn, anyway."

"This is quite a different life from what you're used to."

"There's an understatement."

Will pushed the extension for Letty and asked her to find a dance instructor for Amé. She didn't ask questions, but immediately said she knew just the person and would contact him directly. Will thanked her and told her to call him back as soon as she had a time.

"You certainly know how to get things done," Amé commented.

"*I* don't know how to get things done, so much as I know how to find people who *do*." He smiled. "You will have the same resources available to you." His telephone rang and he excused himself to answer it. It was Letty, telling him that she had gotten in contact with an excellent instructor who would meet Amé in the ballroom the following afternoon at four o'clock.

He told Amé, then asked, "Do you have any other concerns?"

"About a million of them," she said. "But I guess it's all stuff that will get sorted out as we go along."

He nodded. "This leaves the question of how you wish to make the transition from the United States to Lufthania. We can send someone to collect your things, or you can make the journey after the holidays."

"That's fine," she said. "I'd like to go back and do my own packing."

"What do you plan to do about your business?"

"I thought I'd turn it over to Mara. She's been with me for three years and knows the ins and outs as well as I do."

"Excellent. It seems as if you've got it all well in hand. Perhaps your return will not be nearly as traumatic as you feared it would be."

"Maybe not for me," she agreed. "What about for you?"

"For me?"

"You said you plan to leave the palace. Where will you go?"

"To a small château in the country."

She kept her eyes on his. "This is a big place. Can't you just stay here?"

Looking at the beautiful woman before him, her blue eyes soft, her long auburn hair falling so beautifully around her shoulders that it all but begged to be touched, he could well imagine staying. But he couldn't.

"It is impossible."

"Wouldn't look proper, huh?" She looked around the room. "Two people sharing one seventy-five-thousand-square-foot building. Way too intimate."

Although she was kidding, "intimate" was exactly what he was trying to avoid where she was concerned. "I'm sure you can use the extra closet space," he told her.

She gave a hearty laugh. "Clothes are not my weakness. Books, yes. Clothes, no."

He could have guessed that about her already, but it still impressed him. Throughout his bachelorhood, he'd met more clotheshorses than he cared to think about, and that kind of woman left him cold.

It was just one more thing that made Amé so damnably intriguing.

"Then you should be quite happy with the library here. Once you learn German," he added.

She raised an eyebrow. "That may take a while. Do you have a backup plan? Interpreters, maybe?"

"Of course. But you'll need a tutor, of course." He made a note on the pad before him to hire a tutor.

She hesitated, then asked, "What does *Mein herz ist immer hier mit Ihnen* mean?"

The look he gave her was one of shock.

She felt her face grow warm. "Does it mean anything? Did I pronounce it horribly wrong?"

"You pronounced it perfectly," he said slowly.

She waited for him to elaborate, but he just continued to study her with an expression of mingled surprise and what appeared to be sadness.

"Where did you hear it?" he asked after a moment.

"I don't know, I guess it was in a dream. Maybe a memory. Maybe it was something I heard on the television when Letty was watching. Why? What does it mean?" she asked again.

"It means 'My heart is always here with you.'

Chapter Ten

Amy waited alone in the darkened ballroom for the dance instructor to show up. She didn't know how to turn on the lights. Judging from the size of the room, it was probably something that had to be done at some central electrical headquarters somewhere.

She didn't mind. It was actually quite beautiful with the golden afternoon sun slanting through the wall of windows and French doors to the terrace. In the summer that would probably be a beautiful place to sit and watch the sunset, she thought, then it occurred to her that she didn't need to simply imagine it, she could *do* it, if she wanted to. She would be here in the summer.

The idea was still difficult to grasp.

She pictured herself and Will together on the terrace, sipping champagne. Light romantic music played in the background of her imagination. It could be so nice.

Then she remembered that her time now with Will was temporary. He wouldn't be Prince Wilhelm anymore in the summer. And if his coolness toward her the last time she saw him was any indication, he wouldn't be interested in sitting on the terrace or anywhere else with her.

"Amé."

She whirled around, startled. It took her eyes a moment to adjust before she realized it was Will walking toward her.

"What are you doing here in the dark?" he asked.

"Waiting for the dance instructor. Didn't Letty say four o'clock?" She looked at her watch. It was already 4:20 p.m.

"Letty just called and told me that he'd canceled at the last minute. I asked her to come and tell you, but she said she had twisted her ankle and was having a difficult time with the stairs."

Amy frowned. "I saw her after lunch and she was fine."

"She was fine an hour ago as well," he said. Amy couldn't read his expression, but it wasn't a happy one. "Nevertheless, that is what she said."

"So he's not coming."

"Apparently not."

"The ball is in three days."

"Yes."

"And unless I'm allowed to stand on the feet of my

dance partner, I'm going to look like a complete idiot when it's time for me to dance.''

He smiled for the first time in what seemed to her like ages. ''You're going to look a little silly if you stand on his feet as well.''

She laughed. ''You know what I mean.''

He hesitated for a moment, glancing around uneasily, then let out a sigh. ''All right, I'm no teacher, but I'll do what I can.''

''You're going to teach me to waltz?'' She almost laughed. Prince Wilhelm, himself, giving dance instructions. Wait till the girls at the Dentytown Arthur Murray heard about this!

''This is really very simple,'' he said. ''Give me your hand.''

''Which one?''

''Your right.'' He held his arm out. ''Put your hand in mine and the other one on my shoulder.''

Slowly, she lifted her hand to his shoulder and cupped it over the muscled contour. He took her other hand and drew her closer.

Her heart pounded in response.

''Relax,'' he said to her, pressing his hand against her back and gently pulling her closer still. ''You're supposed to look as if you're enjoying yourself.''

''Sorry.'' She swallowed and took a long, slow breath to try to calm down. She couldn't. He was so close. So strong. He smelled so good. And all she could think about was kissing him.

They took a couple of stiff steps, then he stopped.

"Amé." He stepped back. "What's the matter? Do I make you uncomfortable?"

"No," she lied. "It's not you, it's…it's everything else."

He looked puzzled. "What do you mean?"

She hesitated. She couldn't tell him she was uncomfortable because she was falling for him. He'd brought her here hoping she would fall in love with the country, not with him!

"I—I mean," she faltered, "well, look at this place." She opened her arms wide. "I'm not this kind of girl."

"You're not *what* kind of girl?"

"*This* kind. The marble-ballroom, gilded-pillars, French-doors-onto-the-veranda kind of girl. It will take some time to get used to it."

He looked at her for a moment, then asked quietly, "What kind of girl are you?"

Her heart leapt at the low tone of his voice but she tried to keep her answer casual. "You know, I'm from a small town. We don't have great big lives and great big events. Our best Sunday dinner is a roast turkey with stuffing and that's about as big as an event gets."

"Stuffing?" he repeated quizzically.

"Yes, it's bread and celery and onions—some people use sausage or oysters, but don't get me started on *that*. You chop it all up and put it in the breast cavity when you roast a turkey."

"Ah, yes. Dressing." He smiled.

"Yes. Stuffing." She laughed.

"And this precludes you from living comfortably in

the palace?'' There was laughter in his eyes. ''Have the cook add it to the menu.''

She laughed again and said, ''You're humoring me.''

''Is that different from amusing you?''

''Quite.''

''Which do you prefer?''

''*Instruct* me,'' she said. ''I'll relax this time, despite the fact that we have three days until the ball and I have two left feet. I could really do without the humiliation of making a fool of myself in front of a crowd of curious onlookers.''

''You could never look like a fool,'' he said, putting his hand on her shoulder and drawing her in.

''Just you wait,'' she said, a little breathlessly.

He pulled her tighter, placing one hand on her back and taking her hand in his other one. ''Are you ready?''

''As ready as I'm going to be.''

He flashed a quick, heart-stopping white smile and said, ''Step back with your right foot.''

She did and he moved his left foot forward.

''Now bring your left foot next to your right,'' he told her.

He did the same and they continued to move across the dance floor in unison until finally Amy began to feel she was getting the hang of it and relaxed.

''Music would help.''

''I'm afraid I didn't bring an orchestra with me.''

''That was short-sighted of you.'' She smiled.

"You don't need music." He looked deeply into her eyes. "You create your own."

Their movements slowed.

"That's all there is to it."

"I hope I don't forget when I'm on the spot," Amy said.

"You'll do fine," he assured her, letting go of her. "Everyone will love you."

She looked up into his eyes. "Everyone?"

They stopped, but didn't part. "Everyone who matters."

She collected her courage. "Where do you stand in the hierarchy of people who matter?" she asked him.

He adjusted his grip on her hand but didn't let go. "Why do you ask that?"

She drew herself up. "Because ever since finding out that I was truly Princess Amelia, you have been...cooler toward me."

"It's your imagination."

"No, it's not," she said firmly.

He paused, then said, "No, it's not."

She hadn't expected him to agree with her. Somehow that made his rejection even more painful. "So what is it?" she asked, almost afraid to hear the answer. "Did I do something to offend you?"

He responded quickly. "No, of course not, Amé. I'm..." He took a breath. "I'm merely trying to keep our relationship detached."

"Detached?" she repeated.

"Is that the wrong word? I mean impersonal. Professional, you might say."

"But why? I thought we were friends."

"You are the princess of Lufthania. I am merely your subject. One of many."

She couldn't believe he was saying this to her. It was all wrong. "You're the only person here that I know at all. You're the only one I trust to help me."

He looked pained but said, "You can trust anyone on the staff."

"It's not the same. You know it's not the same. I thought we had something together." She threw her pride to the wind. "I thought our relationship was more than just professional. I thought you were my friend."

For one long moment, he looked at her. Finally he shook his head. "You are my monarch."

Like the butterfly, she thought. A delicate thing with a short span of being. "I'm just Amy Scott," she said. "A girl from a small town in Maryland. I'm no monarch."

"Ah, but you are." He started walking toward the French doors to the terrace. "I'm leaving the palace, Amé. I won't be part of this life anymore. It's yours now. Take it."

"So...what?" She called to his back. "You're going to just disappear?"

He turned to face her. "I'm not going to disappear. I'll be close by. But I cannot stay *here*. There's no place for me here."

"You're the *prince*."

"I'm not. I'm a usurper. *You* are the princess, the

only true heir to the throne. It's your time to shine. Now, if you'll excuse me, I must leave.''

"I don't want you to." She hated how forlorn she sounded, but it was the truth. She didn't want him running out on her. She needed him.

She needed him.

Heaven help her. She didn't ever want to need any man again. She was content to be alone. Maybe not deliriously happy, but she at least had the peace of mind that came of not wondering if her life was going to change because of someone else's decision to move on tomorrow. She didn't have to be afraid of getting too attached only to feel the horrible pain of loss because she didn't get too attached.

And yet, here she was, not wanting Will to leave the *room,* much less her life.

Maybe he sensed her desire. Maybe he was trying to distance himself from her before his life was complicated further by their relationship.

He stood before her, looking so regretful that she was about to apologize herself, when he said, "I'm sorry.''

She didn't have time to respond before he turned and started toward the door, in long, purposeful strides.

She was trying to think of something to say to stop him. Anything at all. But all she could think of was that she not only wanted him to stay with her right now, but she wanted him to stay forever.

And there was no way she could confess that to him.

She watched as he approached the door, and she felt more and more empty with every step he took.

Then he stopped.

And he turned around.

Her breath caught in her chest, but she didn't speak. She didn't move. She just waited, with bated breath, to see what he would do next.

She didn't have to wait long. He shook his head and walked back to her. There was no hesitation in his step, no apprehension. He simply strode right up to her, took her in his arms and kissed her.

His mouth was hungry on hers, and he kissed her deeply.

She tipped her head back and drank him in, languishing in his manly scent and in the rough touch of his beard against her skin. This was no polite kiss on the cheek, this was desire so fervent it went beyond words. Desire so urgent it could only be expressed from his lips to hers.

His breath was hot against her skin, making her feel at once safe and dangerous.

She curled her arms around his shoulders and rifled her fingers through the slightly long but wonderfully touchable hair at the nape of his neck. He was a prince, at least for a while, but right now he felt like the rebellious loner, the guy who didn't care about convention or what was proper, who wanted a woman and was willing to shake off whatever conventions might have prevented it.

He was irresistibly attractive.

"Will," Amy breathed as he trailed kisses across

her jaw and down her neck. She nestled against the soft cotton of his collar and wished the moment would never end. "Don't stop."

Wordlessly, he spanned his hands against her lower back and ran his fingers up to her shoulder blades, sending shivers of pleasure up her spine.

Just as she was about ready to shrug out of her shirt entirely and give herself to him, a flash from the direction of the window stopped them both.

"What was that?" she asked.

There was another flash. Her first thought was that it was lightning.

Will shouted an oath, or something that sounded very much like one, in German, and went to the glass doors, throwing them open so that they clattered against their frames.

Amy hurried up behind him. "What was that? Was it a camera?"

"Yes." His voice was grim. "A camera flash. Someone must have told the photographer where we would be."

"But who knew we'd be standing in the dark in the ballroom?"

"I can only think of one person."

Amy looked at him and was about to ask who when it hit her. "No! Not Letty. I can't believe it."

"I wouldn't have suspected her of such a thing, either, but she's been at the center of quite a few incidents lately. She and Christian."

"Like what?"

"Like the telephone line that went dead in your room on your second day here."

"What about it?"

"I went in to fix it and found Christian yanking it out of the wall. He said it was an accident, but I don't believe it. He's worked in the palace far too long to make that kind of mistake."

"But why would he bother?"

"That's what I don't know." Will raked his hand through his hair and paced the floor in front of her. "Why would Letty say she'd hired a dance instructor then call at the last minute to say he wouldn't show up? I would have believed it a coincidence if the photographer hadn't appeared."

"What does Letty have to gain from photos of us...you know, of us kissing? For that matter, how could she even have predicted we would be?"

"Maybe she didn't. Maybe the photographer was trying to get shots of something else. Or maybe he didn't care what he got pictures of, as long as you were in them."

"What's the point of that?"

"I don't know." He stopped in front of her. "I don't know." He shook his head. "It's crazy. It must be a coincidence. Things are often odd when Letty's around."

Amy smiled. "But odd in a good way."

He shrugged. "Perhaps."

"Not in a *bad* way."

He looked in the direction of the doors again. "Not usually."

He was concerned about something but he wasn't going to say what. That made Amy far more nervous than if he had just come right out and told her what it was.

"Is there something we should do?" Amy asked.

He turned to her, clearly distracted. "I'll take care of it. Don't worry. Just stay in the palace. Whatever you do, don't leave. I will find you later."

Without further explanation, he left the room, leaving Amy to stand wondering whether she should be excited or fearful.

Chapter Eleven

"You made the morning paper," Letty announced delightedly, as she walked into Amy's room in the morning, bearing a tray of coffee and pastries and a new edition of the newspaper.

Amy took the paper and shook it open. There, on the front page, was a very large photo of Will and her kissing. The headline beneath shouted Prince and Princess to Marry! in German so clear and obvious that even Amy could comprehend it.

The photo wasn't as unflattering as it could have been. Will looked tall and dark, with a shadow of a beard on his strong, chiseled jaw, and his glossy dark hair falling across his eyes. Amy looked slender in his strong embrace, for which she was grateful, especially after all of the rich food she'd been eating since arriving in Lufthania. Unfortunately, her face was partially visible and, she felt, highly recognizable.

"The two of you look very much in love."

Amy felt her cheeks grow hot, even while a thrill ran through her body at the memory of that kiss. "Letty, we barely know each other."

Letty flicked the newspaper with her finger. "That's not what it looks like to me. Or to the rest of Lufthania."

"Do they really care about this?"

"Indeed they do!" Letty poured some coffee for Amy. "It's been nearly thirty years since Lufthania had a happily married prince and princess on the throne." She looked at Amy with pride. "Your grandparents. God rest their souls."

Amy smiled politely.

Letty went on. "And the people want that romance. We want that happiness to look to. You and Prince Wilhelm could be so good together."

"But we're not *together*."

"And do you not want to be?" Letty lowered her chin and looked at Amy in such a way as to suggest that *of course* she wanted to be with Will and there was no way that Letty would believe anything else.

"It wouldn't matter if I did." She sighed. "He's determined to get as far away from this palace and this role as he can, just as soon as he passes the reins to me." It pained her to say the words aloud, but she knew that she had to accept the truth. He was moving on. Just as everyone else she'd ever cared about had moved on. Better that he was doing it now than waiting until...well, until she was *more* attached.

If that was possible.

"Perhaps he is just frightened, my darling." Letty smoothed Amy's hair back.

"Of what?"

"Of the same things you are. Of loving. Of being loved. Of losing."

How had Letty read all of that in her? "He's a prince, Letty," Amy said, deciding it was easier to focus on Will than on her own fears. "He could have anything he wanted. Why would he be afraid of anything?"

"Because, unfortunately, being a prince, or a princess, doesn't protect you from all of the bad things in life."

Amy nodded. Obviously, her parents' story was proof of that. "But I would imagine that it helped on the romantic front."

Letty shook her head. "Wilhelm was engaged once. To a woman I don't think he truly loved. Not the way he loves now, that is."

"Now?" Amy asked with trepidation. Letty had just suggested that she and Will should be together, but she'd said nothing about love. Yet here she was implying that he *was* in love, which must mean he was in love with someone else.

It was a thought Amy found hard to bear.

Letty chuckled softly. "I mean that he is in love with you, my dear."

Amy's breath left her in one long, relieved rush. "Why do you think so?"

"My dear, I have known that boy since he was ten years old. He was not close to his parents, or his extended family, and he wanted nothing to do with the court or staff of the palace. But he did have a little dog he loved as a child. I knew then that he had the capacity. But I did not see that kind of affection brought out in him again until you arrived."

Amy raised an eyebrow. "So he loves me like a pet dog?"

"No, no, no. I mean only that not since that dog was alive have I seen Wilhelm truly warm toward anyone or anything."

"But he had a fiancée!"

"Yes. Ella. She came from a fine family and it was thought that they would make a good match. But Wilhelm was reluctant to marry her, I think. And the more reluctant he became, the more she clung to him. She was lost in a ski accident after she insisted upon joining him on the slopes of Pirro Mountain." Letty clucked her tongue and shook her head. "It was something she never should have attempted, yet Prince Wilhelm always felt it was his fault."

Amy felt so sorry for both Ella and Will, both for their own separate reasons. "So it's guilt?" she asked. "He didn't love her?"

Letty shook her head. "I'm sorry to say that no, I do not believe he did. But now…" She put her hands on Amy's shoulders. "Now he has a new chance to love. As do you. I hope you won't let this chance slip away."

There was a knock on the door before Amy had a moment to think about that.

"I'll see who it is," Letty said, bustling over to the door.

Amy sipped her coffee and took a thoughtful bite of a croissant. Was it possible that Will really did have feelings for her? Was it possible that the feelings she had for him were genuine, even though they hadn't known each other for very long?

The truth was that ever since she'd arrived in Lufthania, she'd felt at home. It could be argued that it was because she finally *was* home again, and that somewhere in her subconscious she remembered enough of her brief life here to make her feel as if she belonged.

But Amy wasn't so sure that was the whole reason. Since the moment she'd met Will, she'd found something about him intriguing. On the plane ride to Lufthania, he had been charming and funny and even a little bit exasperating. But nothing he'd done had made her feel anything less than fond of him.

As soon as they'd arrived, he'd taken over, confidently commanding the people around him and making sure that everything went smoothly. Part of Amy felt it was a shame he'd be leaving the monarchy, since he was so smooth and competent. But it was probably best that he took those skills to the civil service, where he could truly make a difference. That was, after all, what he wanted to do.

It was her own selfishness that made her want to keep him here.

Or her own love.

"What is the expression?" Letty was asking. "Speak of Satan?"

"Speak of the devil," Amy corrected her, and looked up to see Will making his way in. "Oh, hi."

"I'll just go downstairs and talk to the cook about tonight's menu," Letty said, letting herself out.

Amy looked at Will. "Is something wrong?"

"Everything's fine," he said, sitting down in the chair opposite hers. "I just came to say goodbye."

"Goodbye?" she echoed. "So soon? I thought you were waiting until at least after the ball."

He took a short breath and started to say "This morning," when his eyes landed on the newspaper next to Amy. "You've seen the headlines."

She followed his gaze to the paper, then looked back at him. "Yes, I did. I guess we shouldn't really be all that surprised."

"No," he agreed. "It's not a surprise. But it does complicate things. I'll have to leave sooner than I expected to."

"Because of this?" She picked up the paper and tried to hide her feelings of dismay at the idea of his leaving. "Why? In light of what they're saying, wouldn't it be better if you stayed?"

"Only if what they were saying was the truth."

"But newspapers make things up all the time. That's how they sell copies."

"That's true," he conceded. "But Lufthania is a

country in great need of hope. Ever since my family took over, there has been a sense of fear and unease in this country. The golden days seemed far behind them. I knew that bringing you back would rejuvenate hope and morale for the people, but giving them the impression that we are going to marry and somehow merge our dynasties can only lead to disappointment.''

He wasn't kidding. Amy hadn't been hoping for, or expecting, or even contemplating, a marriage proposal, but his out-of-hand rejection of the idea smarted. ''We wouldn't want to give people the wrong idea,'' she said dryly.

''Exactly.''

''So, tell me, why did you kiss me?'' She didn't bother to point out that he'd done it not once but twice. It was hard enough to be so blunt as to ask, but she wanted to know the answer.

He looked surprised at the question but regained his composure before answering. ''Because you're a beautiful woman. What man wouldn't want to kiss you?''

Under normal circumstances, Amy might have been flattered, but, to the contrary, this felt like a terrible insult. Was that all it had meant to him? ''Are you saying that was all about physical attraction?'' she asked in disbelief. ''And that's all?''

He gave a broad shrug. ''I'm afraid I'm guilty of that, like any man.''

She shouldn't have been surprised. This was precisely the reason she'd tried so hard to resist him. He was a man and men didn't stick around. She thought she was used to it by now, but she still felt the bitter sting of betrayal. "So now you're leaving, not because you don't want the country to get ideas about us but because you don't want *me* to get ideas about us, is that right?" She was rigid with anger.

Something unidentifiable flickered across his expression before he looked at her and said, "I don't want *anyone* to get ideas about us."

Her heart tightened in her chest but she narrowed her eyes at him and said, as coolly as she could manage, "You needn't worry about that."

"Good."

"Now, if you don't have anything further to discuss…?"

"Not at all." He stood up. "I will see you at the ball on Saturday night."

"Yes." There was nothing she could add to that. No matter what she said, it would sound bitter and scornful, and she didn't want to give him the satisfaction of seeing he'd hurt her. Better to hold on to whatever shred of dignity she could, at this point. "Goodbye."

He gave a slight bow. "Goodbye."

She watched him as he turned and, without looking back even once, left her room and the palace that had been his home for twenty-five years.

Will didn't really want to leave, and it wasn't because of the twenty-five years he'd spent living in the palace. He didn't give a damn about that. It wasn't as if he had warm childhood memories of it, or even as if he'd felt he'd accomplished anything particularly worthwhile during his time as crown prince.

No, the reason he didn't want to go was because he didn't want to leave Amy. Yet there was no way he could stay with her, either. He was passing the mantle on to her, not sharing it with her. There was no room in her life for him.

And there was no room in his life for a relationship with her. He wasn't good at love. He couldn't preserve it. Even though he hadn't been in love with Ella, he'd cared about her, and their relationship was the very thing that, in the end, was her downfall.

So, knowing it would be his last day at the palace, Will spent a long day in his office, collecting those things he needed to keep and making arrangements for the relocation of his personal effects.

When he was finally ready to leave, it was after 6:00 p.m.

Franz had stayed on to assist him, and looked profoundly sad when Will announced it was time for him to leave.

"Are you certain about this, sir?" he asked.

Will nodded. "You know as well as I do that it's time for Princess Amelia to take over. We don't belong here anymore."

"You have been a great ruler, Wilhelm," Franz said, uncharacteristically personal.

"I have not been a ruler and you know it." He patted the old man's back. "But we had a good tenure here. And your service has been excellent. I've seen to it that your future is assured."

"Your gesture is appreciated." Franz looked hesitant and Will had the feeling he had more to say.

"What is it, Franz? What's troubling you?"

"It is the princess, sir. There are those who don't feel she has a legitimate claim to be here."

"Who?" Will was instantly on alert. "Have there been threats to her safety?"

"Not precisely. I've only heard, from others on the staff, that some don't feel she belongs here. They might make it difficult for her."

That was something of a relief to Will. A disgruntled staff member was generally less threatening than a disgruntled military leader or politician. "Who has said this to you?" he asked Franz.

"I hate to betray a confidence," Franz began.

"*Who?*"

Franz met his eyes, unintimidated. "I don't know. Gustav has been working in the guardhouse and he has said there are those who want you to remain. That's all I know."

Will believed him. In all the years he'd known the man, he'd never known him to be dishonest.

"I'll speak to him on my way out," Will said, picking up the only item he intended to carry out himself: a small dagger that had been presented to him in private by Prince Josef before his death. At the time, Prince Josef had known his own family was gone and that Will was the future of his country.

Franz held his hand out to Will. "It's been a pleasure serving you, sir," he said, his pale blue eyes watery.

Will took the man's cool, crepey hand in his. "Thank you, Franz."

They looked at each other in silent understanding for a moment before Will turned to leave.

It was a melancholy thing to leave the palace for the last time. The draw back to it was so strong it felt as if he was swimming against the current.

And Amé was the current.

It would have been so easy to stay with her, to stop resisting her pull and give in to it. But he had loved and lost a woman before and it had been difficult to get through. He didn't think it would even be possible to go on if something happened to Amé. Particularly if it was because of his relationship to her.

And that was a very real danger. There were loyalists to his family and loyalists to hers. Few, if any, were loyalists to both. His remaining with Amé could only make her transition to power more difficult.

He shook the thought off. There was no point in continuing to talk himself out of being with her, since there was no question about it. He was leaving. He'd already said his goodbyes. All that was left now was for him to go.

So he did.

The snow was coming down harder now, making the drive from the palace a treacherous one. Will kept his foot on the brake all the way to the guard's station. He stopped there to say goodbye to Gustav, but was surprised to find that no one was there.

He put the car in Park and took out his mobile phone to call Franz.

"Do you have any idea why there is no guard at the gate?" he asked when Franz answered.

"No, sir. I gave strict orders for increased security."

"I'm coming back," Will said, more to himself than to Franz. Something wasn't right. He didn't know what it was, but he had a bad feeling and he wasn't going to leave Amé unprotected in the palace as long as he felt that way.

He turned the vehicle around and headed back toward the palace.

Would he never be able to leave her, he wondered as the thought of Amé drew him closer.

She was impossible. Absolutely impossible. But she was so lively and beautiful that he couldn't get her out of his thoughts. He had a thousand snapshots of her in his mind already: laughing in the snow, dancing in the afternoon light in the ballroom, talking to Herr George in town. She had seemed so at home here.

And, perhaps even more amazingly, she had made him feel at home.

Why did he have the terrible feeling that he might lose her?

He hurried into the palace, nearly knocking Christian over in his haste.

"Is something wrong?" Christian asked. "Is the princess all right?"

Will stopped short. "Why do you ask that?"

"I just saw Gustav on his way to her room," Christian said, looking worried. "He had his gun drawn."

Will muttered an oath. "It's Gustav," he said urgently. "Call the guards to the princess's quarters immediately. Warn them that he's armed."

"Is she all right?" Christian asked, his voice fretful and small as Will rapidly increased the distance between them.

"I hope so." If Christian said anything else, Will didn't hear him. There was no time for him to stop to reassure Christian now.

Will ran through the hallways and stopped in front of Amé's door. He didn't have a plan. If he burst in, he ran the risk of startling an armed man, which could result in catastrophe. But if didn't act quickly, there could be a catastrophe, anyway.

Time won out. He gave a warning cough and pushed the door open.

When he saw Gustav there, holding a gun on Amé, his heart lurched. It took some effort but he managed to keep from lunging at the man immediately.

"What's going on here?" he asked in German, trying to sound more curious than alarmed.

"There was an intruder, sir," Gustav said in thick English, giving Will a conspiratorial nod. He was obviously trying to rattle Amé by alerting him to his plans. "As soon as I realized it, I came in to save the princess, but, alas, it was too late." He leveled the gun at Amé.

She gasped and looked pleadingly at Will.

"Wait," he said to Gustav, not meeting her eyes for fear of giving all of his feelings away, even to a brainless lunk like Gustav. "Are you sure no one saw you come in?"

"That old goat Christian saw me, but he's easily taken care of. I'll tell him I saw an intruder."

"Ah, good thinking," Will said in his most approving manner. "Very well, go ahead and—" He stopped short. "Wait." He said it in German, to be sure that Gustav understood him. "The draperies are open. With all the press Amelia has been getting lately, you might well have witnesses with cameras directly outside the window. It's already happened once." He remembered the kiss pictured in the newspaper and hoped to God he'd have the opportunity to kiss her again.

Gustav stopped and gave a wild-eyed glance toward the window. "You're right."

"Give me the gun," Will said, extending his hand. "You close the drapes."

For a moment, Gustav appeared to consider it. Will couldn't believe it was that easy.

It wasn't.

Gustav's expression turned suspicious. "You close them," he said, holding the gun steadily on Amé.

It was important to remain calm. To look as if he was wholly on Gustav's side. "I always knew your allegiance to my family was strong," Will said, walking slowly. "If only the rest of the staff were as loyal as you are."

"They're weak," Gustav said. "Every one of them."

Thank God. He was working alone. Will caught Amé's eye and gave the slightest nod.

"The strongest army begins with one man," Will commented.

"Yes, sir."

Will closed the drapes, trying to buy time. "Tell me something else, Gustav. Is there anyone waiting for you at home? Someone who will serve as an alibi for you this evening?"

"I live alone," Gustav said. "I wouldn't have it any other way."

"I felt that way once," Will said, then in English added, "Then I fell in love and everything I thought I knew turned out to be wrong." He met Amé's eyes and saw them soften.

"Why are you talking in English?" Gustav demanded.

"Why make our visitor feel left out?" Will walked behind Amé and put his hands on her shoulders in a way that he hoped looked menacing but felt comforting. "Who is she going to tell?"

Gustav nodded. "She'll tell no one."

"As I said, I fell in love. But I pushed her away, thinking I was doing what was best for her and for Lufthania." He gave Amé's shoulders a gentle squeeze. "I was wrong. And by the time I realized it, it seemed it was too late."

"You're talking about Frauline Ella," Gustav said, lowering the gun for just a moment.

It was just long enough for Will to leap at him and try to wrench it free. The struggle that took place took longer than Will imagined it would. Gustav was still in fine shape, and his hatred for Amé and her family seemed to fire his adrenaline.

Will grabbed the man's wrist and squeezed it, trying to make him drop the gun, but Gustav resisted, trying to raise his arm to level it on Amé.

Enraged that the man might actually fire at her, Will wrenched Gustav's arm back and took the gun. Somehow in the struggle, it fired, an explosion that rang through Will's ears and brought the acrid smell of sulfur to his nostrils. It wasn't until he saw the blood pouring from his leg that he realized he'd been hit.

Adrenaline surged and he pulled the gun free, stumbled backward and fired at Gustav, hitting him in the chest just as the palace guards burst in.

He didn't care what happened to Gustav from that point on. All he cared about, all he could see, was Amé. He went to her and untied her hands.

"Oh, Will!" She threw her arms around him.

"Amé." He held her tight. "I don't know what I would have done if anything had happened to you."

"Are you really in love? With me?"

He kissed her. "More in love than I ever dreamed I could be."

Tears poured down her cheeks. "I'll stay," she promised. "No matter what happens, I'll stay here with you." She shifted her weight, accidentally knocking his leg.

He moaned with pain and she looked down and saw what had happened. "My God, you've been hit!" she cried.

As soon as she said it, two guards rushed over to him.

"He's losing a lot of blood," one of them said in German.

"It hit an artery!" the other shouted. "Call for help."

The last thing Will heard before he blacked out was Amé saying to him, "Don't you leave me now that I've promised to stay. I love you, Will. Don't leave me!"

He reached for her hand and murmured, "Never. I will never leave you. My heart is here with you always."

Epilogue

"Ladies and gentlemen, it was my intention to introduce you this evening to your new princess, Amelia. But something has happened and I have an even more exciting announcement to make."

A hush came over the crowd.

Amy stepped forward, her limbs trembling, until Will took her hand.

"Tonight I present to you Princess Amelia," he announced. "And my bride-to-be."

The crowd erupted in cheers and shouts of congratulations in both German and English.

"When's the wedding?" someone called in English.

Will looked at Amé and gave a small nod. "On Sunday the twenty-fifth of this month."

"You will all, of course, be there," Will said with a laugh. "Invitations or no."

Laughter trickled across the room.

"Will you remain Prince Wilhelm?" someone asked, and the crowd quieted to hear the answer.

Will shook his head. "I do not have the bloodline for the throne of Lufthania," he said. "But my children will." He looked at Amé and she beamed up at him.

The cheers erupted again.

"Now, it would be traditional at this time for the princess to have the first dance and commence the ball, but she has decided she would rather stay with her hobbled fiancé while the rest of you enjoy the dance." He indicated the crutch he was using while the bullet wound in his leg healed, then smiled at his bride. "She's very stubborn, so we should all get used to the fact that our traditions are about to change."

"For the better," she added quickly.

The guests clapped and several of them called, "Welcome home, Amelia."

At Will's signal, the band began to play and the people crowded onto the dance floor.

"There, see?" Amé said. "You don't *have* to do things a certain way just because you always have."

"I'm learning that all the time." He took her hand in his. "I spoke with the pilot just before we came in here. Your parents will arrive by midnight."

She smiled broadly. "My mother is going to drive me crazy with wedding plans."

"Would you prefer to elope?"

"She'd kill me. She wants a huge ceremony. I think she imagines it will even be televised."

"Then a huge ceremony it will be," he said. "Right here at the palace. Invite all of your friends and family. They can all stay at the palace with us that week."

"Are you serious?"

"Amé, I want everyone in the world to know how I feel about you. I'll have a wedding every week if you want."

She laughed. "I don't think *that* will be necessary."

"Whatever it takes," he said, bending down to kiss her. "You are my heart, and I want the world to know it."

*   *   *   *   *

If you enjoyed what you just read,
then we've got an offer you can't resist!

Take 2 bestselling love stories FREE!

Plus get a FREE surprise gift!

///////////////////////

Clip this page and mail it to Silhouette Reader Service

IN U.S.A.	IN CANADA
3010 Walden Ave.	P.O. Box 609
P.O. Box 1867	Fort Erie, Ontario
Buffalo, N.Y. 14240-1867	L2A 5X3

YES! Please send me 2 free Silhouette Romance® novels and my free surprise gift. After receiving them, if I don't wish to receive anymore, I can return the shipping statement marked cancel. If I don't cancel, I will receive 6 brand-new novels every month, before they're available in stores! In the U.S.A., bill me at the bargain price of $21.34 per shipment plus 25¢ shipping and handling per book and applicable sales tax, if any*. In Canada, bill me at the bargain price of $24.68 plus 25¢ shipping and handling per book and applicable taxes**. That's the complete price and a savings of at least 10% off the cover prices—what a great deal! I understand that accepting the 2 free books and gift places me under no obligation ever to buy any books. I can always return a shipment and cancel at any time. Even if I never buy another book from Silhouette, the 2 free books and gift are mine to keep forever.

209 SDN DU9H
309 SDN DU9J

Name	(PLEASE PRINT)	
Address	Apt.#	
City	State/Prov.	Zip/Postal Code

* Terms and prices subject to change without notice. Sales tax applicable in N.Y.
** Canadian residents will be charged applicable provincial taxes and GST.
   All orders subject to approval. Offer limited to one per household and not valid to
   current Silhouette Romance® subscribers.
   ® are registered trademarks of Harlequin Books S.A., used under license.

SROM03   ©1998 Harlequin Enterprises Limited

COMING NEXT MONTH

#1714 THE PIED PIPER'S BRIDE—Myrna Mackenzie
The Brides of Red Rose

The women of Red Rose needed men—and they'd decided sexy Chicago bigwig Parker Monroe was going to help find them! But Parker wasn't interested in populating his hometown with eligible bachelors. Enter their secret weapon, Parker's former neighbor. But how was the love-shy Ellie Donahue supposed to entice her former crush to save the town without sacrificing her heart a second time?

#1715 THE LAST CRAWFORD BACHELOR—
Judy Christenberry
From the Circle K

Assistant District Attorney Michael Crawford was perfectly happy being the last unmarried Crawford son and he didn't need Daniele Langston messing it up. But when Dani aroused his protective instincts, his fetching co-*worker* became his co-*habitant.* Now this business-minded bachelor was thinking less about the courtroom and more about the bedroom….

#1716 DADDY'S LITTLE MEMENTO—Teresa Carpenter

The only convenient thing about Samantha Dell's marriage was her becoming a stepmother to precious eleven-month-old nephew Gabe. Living with Gabe's seductive reluctant daddy didn't work into her lifelong plans. *And getting pregnant by him?* Well, that certainly wasn't part of the arrangement! Would falling in love with her heartthrob husband be next?

#1717 BAREFOOT AND PREGNANT—Colleen Faulkner

Career-driven Ellie Montgomery had everything a girl could want—except a husband! But *The Husband Finder* was going to change that. Except, according to the book, her perfect match, former bad-boy Zane Keaton, was definitely Mr. Wrong! But a few of Zane's knee-weakening, heart-stopping kisses had Ellie wondering if he might be marriage material after all.

SRCNM0304